The
PETTICOAT PARTY

Go West,
Young Women!

The
PETTICOAT PARTY
Book 1

Go West, Young Women!

KATHLEEN KARR

HarperTrophy®
A Division of HarperCollinsPublishers

Harper Trophy® is a registered trademark of
HarperCollins Publishers Inc.

Library of Congress Cataloging-in-Publication Data
Karr, Kathleen.
    Go west, young women! / Kathleen Karr.
        p.   cm. — (Petticoat party book one)
    Summary: When a disaster claims the men of their wagon train, spunky
twelve-year-old Phoebe, her mother, sister, and the other women rely on
their own resources to complete the journey to Oregon in 1846.
    ISBN 0-06-027151-5. — ISBN 0-06-027152-3 (lib. bdg.)
ISBN 0-06-440495-1 (pbk.)
    [1. Overland journeys to the Pacific—Fiction.   2. Sex role—Fiction.
3. Women—West (U.S.)—Fiction.]   I. Title.   II. Series: Karr, Kathleen.
Petticoat Party book one.
PZ7.K149Go   1996   95-25060
[Fic]—dc20   CIP
                                                                  AC

Typography by Steve M. Scott
❖
First Harper Trophy edition, 1997

For Iris—a friend as steadfast as my pioneers

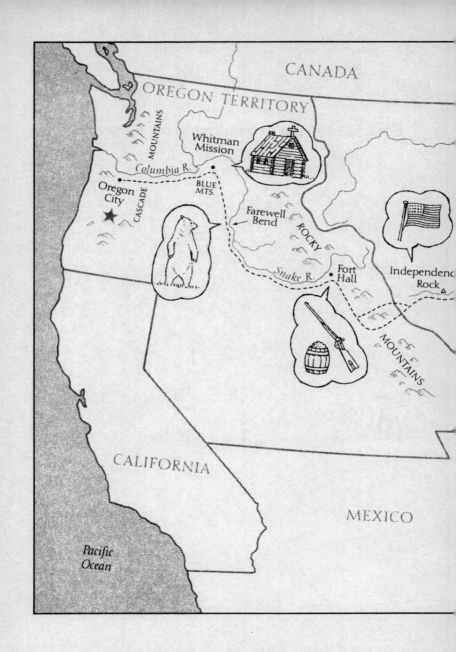

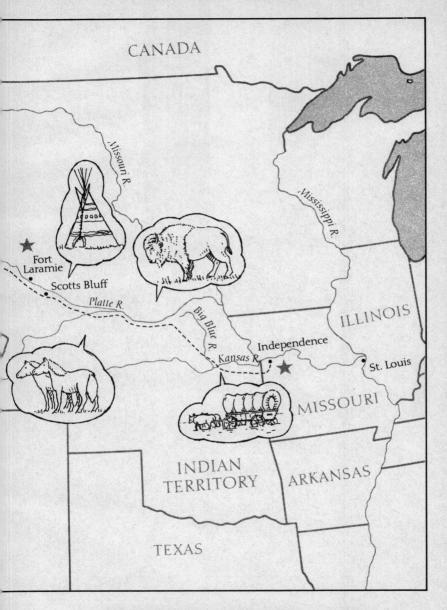

THE OREGON TRAIL: 1846

ONE

*D*isaster never would have struck if the gunpowder hadn't been drenched in that river crossing so early on. The Kansas River, it was—in full flood. Those cold waters weren't particularly beneficial to our provisions, either. But by the time the true damage was assessed, it was too late to turn back. Entirely too late.

The whole journey had become a comedy of errors, but it was hard to laugh with a rumbling stomach. That's why the men got so excited by the first buffalo and . . .

But maybe this story ought to begin at the beginning.

Papa got the urge to see the elephant the winter of 1845. That expression had nothing to do with true elephants, which I could have understood, never having laid eyes on one of *them* myself. It meant, instead, he'd developed a strong itch to see vast new wonders. It meant he wanted to move west to the Oregon Country, badly. And when Papa wanted to do something, the rest of us had no say in the matter.

Granted, our Massachusetts farm wasn't anything to brag about. It couldn't hold a candle to what newspapers were claiming for Oregon's Willamette Valley: man-tall grass green four seasons sprouting from loam a yard thick. Our land was mostly rock, and Papa'd already shipped my big sister Amelia off to work in the mills in Lowell the summer before—over Mama's piteous entreaties about how the oldest family in the community didn't indenture their daughters to *labor*.

"*Oldest* has never signified *wealthiest*, Ruth," Papa countered. "The farm just isn't supporting all of us anymore." The deed was done.

Amelia sent her wages home diligently, then came home herself at Christmas, declaring she'd never go back. That rankled Papa.

"You are seventeen years old, and unmarried," he said. "I am not beholden to feed you forever, Amelia. Particularly with your newfound appetite."

"Well, then find me a husband, Papa, if you can!"

That stopped him cold right there at the dinner table.

Amelia wasn't exactly a raving beauty, especially since she'd gained about fifty pounds from

homesickness and Lowell boardinghouse pota-
toes. I tried to remember her before Lowell and
the extra weight. Maybe there had been some
promise, given time and a beneficent Providence.
Now her dark brown hair remained full and lovely,
and her enormous brown eyes could still sparkle
when they inspected Mama's laden dinner table.
But the only young man who'd ever taken notice
was Tom Horner, and he'd gone after the whales a
year back and was probably stiff as a corpse in
Greenland by this time.

Papa turned to me. I shuddered.

"Since none of you even wants to *think* about
Oregon"—he considered me thoughtfully—"perhaps
it is time, Ruth, for Phoebe to do her share."

Alarmed, Mama raised her eyes from her plate.
"Phoebe has yet to finish her schooling. She is but
twelve, Henry. Delicate and undersized—"

I slid down in my chair, trying to appear as
small as possible. To emphasize the point I pulled a
hank of my long auburn hair around my face.
Naturally pale cheeks became suddenly hollow by
dint of sucking them in. I blinked my green eyes as
waifishly as I could.

"Surely," Mama continued, "surely the mills
would not accept a child for the work?"

Amelia snatched another plump biscuit from

the serving plate. "There were several nine-year-olds on my floor, Mama."

Some destinies were worse than others. Amelia had been telling me about those satanic weaving machines that regularly consumed fingers, and worse. And the twelve-and-three-quarter-hour work days—six days a week—with the mill bell that woke the "operatives" long before dawn. I'd even found protest pamphlets hidden under her mattress. Curious tracts, titled *The Evils of Factory Life*, or *Lowell Slavery*, neatly printed, and signed only "Amelia."

I choked on the mutton, gone dry and forgotten in my mouth. My cheeks puffed out again, and I flexed all ten of my fingers, as if to verify the mere threat of Lowell hadn't severed any of them. Quick thinking was required to divert Papa and save myself.

"They say *any* woman can get a husband in Oregon, Papa," I remarked. "And isn't neighbor Jenkins seeking to expand his properties? He could afford ours, too, since he married that rich widow."

Papa's fork clattered onto his plate as he rose from the table. "I'll have my pie later, Ruth."

Dusty, jarring trains and steamboats whose boilers seemed about one gasp from explosion got us to Independence, Missouri, in late March. Independence was the staging point for all the dreamers benighted enough to want to go farther west. It looked like nothing so much as the armpit frontier of the world, lacking as it did few refinements other than wagon building and provisioning establishments. Half-tame Indians strolled at their ease down the mud streets in trade blankets and feathers. Unwashed, bearded men—gamblers, Santa Fe muleteers, and slaves—mixed in Courthouse Square.

Yet armpit or not, beyond Independence was only that vast, blank area an obliging teacher had pointed out on a map during my last week at the Young Ladies' Seminary. "The American Desert," she assured me, "is a lunar surface of precipice and volcanic sterility." In short, beyond Independence was *nothing*.

Papa tarried a few weeks organizing our westering equipment, primary among which was a canvas-topped wagon about ten feet long, five feet wide, and two feet deep. Even fortified with strap iron and iron-rimmed wheels, it was an unprepossessing object to serve as home for the next six months. He finally signed us on with a small wagon train and we left civilization on a cold, wet day in April. Mama cried.

← «»» →

Amelia and I were determined that anything was better than the mills. That became debatable after several days of trudging in mud halfway up our legs, either pulling or whipping our poor oxen. Who'd have thought a lunar surface could be this wet and sticky?

It didn't help that my sister and I had to sleep on that very surface under the wagon bed to keep out of the rains. There just wasn't enough room for us inside. It was true that the rims supporting the canvas of the whitetop were high enough that a body could stand upright under the center arch, but our earthly belongings were packed more than four feet high on either side. The narrow passage left down the middle of the wagon barely allowed room for Mama and Papa to rest. None of us were getting a whole lot of that.

We didn't meet many of our fellow sufferers till the weather started clearing, about the third day on the trail. The train had twelve wagons, and a captain. George Kennan had been elected leader by the other men before leaving Independence. The men had even written up and signed an official Constitution, just like the one governing the United States. It set out all the things that were agreed to in case of eventualities—mainly that the emigrants would stick together and help each other, come hell or high water, straight through to the Oregon Country. But we had no proper guide, because all the men were trying to save their money for Oregon.

Kennan swore there wasn't anything to it. He'd bought a guidebook, hadn't he? All we had to do was follow the tracks of those gone before us. The men agreed with Kennan. The women were of other minds on the subject.

Some of these minds presented themselves to us as Mama, Amelia, and I tried to ignite a supper fire with damp wood that third evening. Captain Kennan's wife, Tabitha, slogged through muddy wheel tracks, skirts hiked almost to her knees, to borrow some fire.

"I did pack my lucifers, Mrs. Brown, but I just can't seem to find them!"

Mama wasn't having much luck with the match in her own hand. As the sulphur crumbled upon itself, she let out an unusual sigh of exasperation. "Oh! How one is to remain genteel in this wilderness escapes me. To think I left behind hearth, home, church, and community for this, this *chimera*!"

"A woman's lot is a hard one, indeed, Mrs. Brown. I try daily to impress it upon my girls."

"You have daughters, too, Mrs. Kennan?" A new spark of interest lit Mama's green eyes as she shoved a wisp of brown hair back into her bun. She'd found a kindred spirit.

"Call me Tabitha, please. Indeed, I do. Two strapping twins. Hannah! Sarah!"

They came on the run, and the four of us younger females took each others' measure. The Kennan twins were of an age between Amelia and me. Perhaps fifteen. And they were, indeed, strapping. Their maturity blossomed forth in calico straining at their chests. Any more maturity and that cloth would be losing the battle. Glancing down at my own flat chest, I hardly even noticed the matching blond braids, or the perfectly chiseled noses and heart-shaped ovals of their delicate matching faces. Amelia noticed everything. Already she was tucking in her stomach, trying to hide her double chin. Thus we stood in uncomfortable silence until another woman strode up.

"Having trouble with the fire, are you? It'll be needing dry tinder. Here, I brought some." She thrust a handful of straw upon our chosen hearth, snatched a fresh match from Mama's fluttering fingers, and in a moment had a blaze going. It outlined the newcomer's gray bun and fleshy features against dark storm clouds building again on the prairie horizon. "Hepzibah Hawkins. My husband calls me Happy. Sometimes. When he's not up in arms about this journey."

"You mean"—Mama breathed in awe—"you mean, you came of your own volition?"

"Had the devil of a time uprooting Theodore from his 'ancestral lands,' as he called them. If they're that ancestral, I says, ain't it time to be passing them on to our sons? Before they have to plow over our bones to get them? We're still spry enough, says I. Let's try finding some lands with a little promise, like starting over newly married."

Mama and Mrs. Kennan stared at that woman as if she were a cholera carrier. I had to break the moment, out of courtesy. Amazing for Mama to forget courtesy.

"Are there any others like you in the train, Mrs. Hawkins?"

She slapped the well-padded rear section of her anatomy and roared. "There be the Davises and the Russells nearly our age—too old to be carting youngsters—but both menfolk have the upper hand." She laughed again. "Nope. Happy Hawkins is the only anathema on this here train, I'll be bound."

"Anomaly," Amelia corrected in a whisper. "Meaning different from the rest." Perhaps the

Young Ladies' Literary Society of Lowell had done more than compose tracts.

Mrs. Hawkins's bright bird eyes swiveled around. "What's that, dearie?"

Tabitha Kennan had been holding a switch in our new fire. Now she pulled it out, blazing. "Come along, daughters. There'll be months for better acquaintance. Your father expects his supper in a timely manner, wilderness or no."

An ominous rumble in the swiftly blackening sky got the rest of us moving. Mrs. Hawkins paused just long enough to fix those eyes on Amelia again. "I'll be knowing what an anathema is, dearie. It's a soul what's been cursed. And haven't I been cursed with the desire to travel all my born days? Well, now Happy Hawkins is doing her traveling at long last. And I aim to enjoy every moment of it!"

The rain came, and I ran for the family umbrella to shield our struggling supper fire.

There seemed an inordinate number of women on that train, and a singular lack of men. Young men, that is, as Amelia and the twins began to point out with tedious regularity. Had most of the husbands present chosen the way west as some kind of compensation for not fathering sons? Or had they purposely emigrated to find ready-made husbands for their excess of daughters? That there were excess females in the East had been driven home to us by Papa on many earlier occasions.

"The call of the sea and the city is draining the countryside of eligible males," Papa would moan as he studied Amelia and me. "Unfortunately, convents are not an American solution," he'd add ruefully. "Although the mills do seem to be addressing part of the situation. . . ."

As Amelia and I had already foresworn the latter and had little interest in the former, we tried to keep Papa content on the trail. We worked hard to create breakfast pancakes that wouldn't stick to the frying pan and burn over the uneven heat of the campfire. We labored mightily not to singe his dinner bacon or his supper beans. In between times we walked with him next to the oxen, leaving only Mama to jounce queasily on the hard seat of the wagon. We learned to catch and yoke the beasts in the morning and set them free at the nooning.

The other girls were doing the same. Besides the twins, there were the three daughters of the Beckers— all younger than I—and the four daughters of the O'Malleys. You couldn't miss those O'Malleys. The whole lot of them had hair the color of carrots newly pulled from a kitchen garden. And freckles, so many that I'd even seen Margaret O'Malley—the one my age—teaching her little brother his numbers by counting the freckles on his arm. Yes, the O'Malleys were blessed in that their fifth child was a son. Young Timothy was the apple of his family's eye, and at the tender age of four had become a terror from the attention.

Rounding out our party were three younger couples, as yet unencumbered by offspring, and Zachary Judd, a middle-aged bachelor on his own. Lastly, there were the real anomalies of the trip— two maiden ladies so besotted by the idea of wilderness that they'd hired a drover to take them over the two-thousand-mile Oregon Trail. Miss Simpson and Miss Prendergast kept to their own devices. It was not until much later that we began to appreciate their unique qualities.

On the eighth day we came to our first major river crossing: the Kansas. Captain Kennan had gathered the men together the evening before for a "planning session," as he called it. According to Papa's report, Kennan—after consulting his guide-book—assured all that there would be a genuine ferry on the Kansas River to ease us across, for a fee.

Somewhere during the course of the next morning, however, Captain Kennan chose to follow the wrong set of tracks. When we arrived on the banks of the Kansas, there was no ferry to greet us. Nor was there sign of one in any direction. Mama creaked anxiously on her wagon seat.

"Henry?" She paused to delicately remove a splinter from the seat of her nether quarters. "Henry. Ought not Captain Kennan send a man to scout for the ferry?"

Papa frowned. "Don't fuss, Ruth. Kennan knows what to do. Besides, the toll he quoted last night was exorbitant."

An early halt was called for the nooning, and the entire party walked to the edge of the river and gingerly leaned over its banks to assess the situation.

It was fuller than the Merrimack during spring flood. And wilder. Next to me, Amelia's eyes grew as large as her appetite. She gripped my arm until it pained me.

"I don't want to die, Phoebe! Not now. Not before I've had a *chance* at a husband!"

I pried her fingers loose and rubbed at the red marks on my forearm. "I'm surprised you've still an interest in the gender, sister, considering where it's brought us."

"Oh, but I *have!*" she wailed. "They can't all be like Captain Kennan and Papa!"

I studied the suicidal waters before us. "That remains to be seen."

Captain Kennan let out a hale and hearty shout, as if the raging torrent presented not a single problem, and began tying ropes to a tree to winch the first wagon into the river, oxen foremost. It was not a pretty sight watching the Beckers' whitetop slough into the waters of their doom.

The three Becker girls—Greta, Zelda, and Hetty—poked their heads out of the rear opening. They were holding on to the canvas so tightly I half expected it to shred under their fingers. Mr. Becker slashed at his oxen with his whip. The beasts—already up to their flanks in the river—went crazy. Instead of swimming across the currents, they jerked to the right and took off, hauling the wagon with them. Horned heads disappeared beneath the waters to bob up again, much farther downstream. This pattern continued, each submersion of the beasts dragging the whitetop partially underwater. By the time the Hawkinses' wagon had been winched to the river's edge, the Becker wagon was gone east, around a bend and out of sight. The rest of us turned accusing glares on Captain Kennan.

He tugged at his thick moustache. "We'll give them aid and succor on the other side."

The Hawkinses made it across. Mrs. Hawkins had taken the whip from her terrified husband. Learning from the Beckers, she nudged rather than spooked the oxen. The whitetop sank below its sideboards only once, then the wagon was hauled up the far side. Thus it went, wagon after wagon, all making it across with a minimum of submersions. Until it was our turn.

Lots had been pulled for the crossing, and ours was the last. Mama had fainted dead away after the Beckers disappeared around the bend, and was still sprawled out atop the feather beds inside the musty wagon. Amelia, a mass of palpitating flesh, was huddled in the narrow corridor by her feet. I wasn't anxious for a cold bath, but someone had to sit next to Papa on the wagon seat and pray for deliverance. I did my duty.

When the first waters struck my legs I knew for a certitude that Reverend Bean at the First Congregational Church back home had been wrong. Hell was not hot. It was *cold*. When the river came over the sideboards, right up to my waist, I judged the Kansas had been misnamed. It was the River Jordan in disguise, and ready or not, I was about to meet my Maker.

I managed to open my eyes long enough to focus on the wrathful deluge yet before us. The far side didn't appear to be overflowing with milk and honey. No matter. We'd never make it to those sandy banks anyway. Under the canvas behind me, the flooding waters had woken Mama. Her groans blended with Amelia's shrieks. It was the perfect orchestration for a final examination of my conscience.

I had not excelled in my needlework. I had concealed myself beneath my warm quilt, allowing Mama to spare me from milking the cows on frigid winter mornings. I had refused to master the intricacies of a good pudding. I had not shown sufficient concern for my elder sister's troubles. I had hidden too often with a book, leaving Mama to scrub the floors. I had driven the teachers at the Young Ladies' Seminary to distraction with my parsing of Latin verbs. I had not even tried to understand Papa's attempts at bettering the lot of our family. Worst of all, *I had refused to go to Lowell.* My sins were being punished.

It will all change, Lord. I promise— Frigid water splashed my eyes, forcing them open.

"Phoebe! Grab the whip! I have to wade ashore."

"Yes, Papa. What? We made it?"

"And try to stop that caterwauling in the rear. It's more than a man can take."

"Yes, Papa."

TWO

*A*melia and Mama and I began to wring out
and dry everything we owned. Papa and
the other men went in search of the Beckers and
loose livestock.

The men were gone a long while. They were
gone so long that Amelia and I had time to make
rock-hard pan bread from some of the gooey flour
in the grain barrel. They were gone so long that
Mama had time to cry herself dry over what the
Kansas River had done to Grandmother Wintle's
cherrywood highboy chest of drawers. That chest—
sitting side by side in two neat halves—had been
taking up all the space not used by necessaries in
our wagon. Mama had refused to leave Massachusetts without it. Now Mama, red-eyed, rubbed it
again and again with beeswax and a cloth she'd
dried over our fire—the fire we wouldn't have had if
the match safe hadn't been wrapped in greased,
waterproofed linen. Too bad that dresser hadn't
been wrapped up, too. Mama and the chest would

never be the same. The finer veneers were lifting on both of them.

Papa returned way past dark. He sank down by the fire, grabbed a piece of bread, and promptly cracked a tooth on it. Amelia and I watched silently as he spat bread and tooth into the flames. His head rose slowly on a neck strong and tough as oak. A hand exploded through his dark, grizzled hair. His solid body swiveled slowly between the two of us.

"The Beckers aren't joining us. They fished themselves out, right back on the south side of the Kansas. They shouted across the river that they were alive, but had enough. The wagon was lost, and all but one ox. They're heading back to New York."

Amelia poured a tin cup full of coffee. "Try dunking the bread in it, Papa."

I pulled my dank blanket closer to the fire and attempted to sleep. We hadn't even had time to get properly acquainted with those Becker girls. Next to me the wagon complained, its boards still oozing Kansas River.

Our Manifest Destiny didn't look much better the next morning. I'd asked the Kennan twins—

during an earlier morning on the dry side of the Kansas—what that phrase meant, because the captain had it painted all over the side of his whitetop.

Hannah had shrugged. "Our daddy's a patriot."

"It means," clarified Sarah, "that as Americans we have the right and duty to expand our borders as far as they'll go."

"All the way to the Oregon Country," finished Hannah.

"Oh." I pondered the information. "I thought the point of the journey was free land."

"Daddy believes in free land, too, Phoebe. Indeed, he does."

"And men in need of wives, Sarah, never forget that," Hannah added.

They'd both been brushing their golden hair prior to braiding it for the road. Sarah admired herself in a little hand mirror before sharing it with her sister. "I'm not about to forget that, Hannah. Indeed, I'm not."

Now, in the first light of the rising prairie sun, the bold lettering on Captain Kennan's wagon was still dripping from its bath in the Kansas. The legs of the *M* on *Manifest* oozed clear to the bottom edge of the canvas, as if groping for soil to root in.

I shivered. It was too much like a sign.

We journeyed an entire week past the Kansas River and it didn't rain even once. The prairie spread out flatter and drier around us. Grass was greening and tiny flowers were sprouting everywhere. It was pretty, with the sky so blue, and the horizon so clear. A body could see almost forever, not just to the edge of the nearest hills, like in Massachusetts. We were making good time, too—a fairly steady fifteen miles a day. We'd become more efficient about our nooning chores, and our wheels weren't getting grounded in muck every other mile.

Things would have augured well if we hadn't noticed strange stirrings in our provisions. Amelia and I were having a harder and harder time scraping flour out of the barrel. It had just been wet and gooey after the river crossing. Now it had turned harder than a cone of salt, with curiously colored veins growing through it. The beans had all begun to sprout. The bacon had developed thick crusts of green mold. And maggots.

It was the last that most impressed Amelia. She inspected the meat one morning, became green herself, and turned to me. "I do believe I shall fast today, Phoebe."

I watched her run off into a private piece of prairie to be sick. Taking another look at the provisions, it occurred to me that perhaps we'd all be better for fasting this day.

Papa was not of the same mind. "Scrape off the extras, Phoebe, and cook what's left. Waste not, want not."

After another week of scraping off the extras there wasn't much *left*. Amelia began to look different, too, I noticed one forenoon as I trailed behind her. Gone was the heavy, plodding walk. She moved more nimbly, with the beginnings of grace. And when she turned her head, I could detect a subtle difference in her double chin.

Soon thereafter, Papa began to keep a serious lookout for wildlife.

"Where's my rifle, Ruth? Three rabbits just crossed my path. They were still spring thin, but tempting nevertheless."

"In the middle drawer of Mother's cherry chest, Henry."

I watched Papa crawl into the slowly moving wagon and heard an ill-concealed oath as he banged his knee against a sharp edge of Mama's pride and joy. Another oath came as he struggled to pull open the warped drawer.

"You may leave God out of it, Henry," Mama placidly commented from her seat. "*He* set a ferry upon the Kansas for our intelligent use."

"*He* didn't order up cherry highboys as standard westering equipment!" Papa barked back.

"*He* favored us with sufficient food and a comfortable home in Massachusetts."

The drawer shot out against Papa's shins. I heard him count slowly to ten. "*He* also favored us with daughters instead of sons. Daughters for whom I am trying to seek a future."

Papa stumbled out of the wagon's rear, rifle in hand. Mama reached for her Bible. Then Papa jogged forward with a new thought.

"The shot, Ruth. And the powder?"

Mama glanced up sweetly from her book. "The shot is in the top drawer of the chest, Henry. And the powder keg should be to the left of the chest, under the feather beds and the beans."

Papa chased after the lumbering wagon, squinting through the rear opening. He was reckoning on his chances with the monster chest. "It will keep till the nooning," he decided.

We rolled on.

Papa choked on a mouthful of his dinner. "If I wanted *salat* to eat, I could hunker down to the grass like the oxen."

I glanced at the sprouting beans in my own

dish. Even the molasses didn't cover up the empty bean shells. The pods had looked rather amusing for the first week. Their shoots had been all green and sprightly, stretching for sunlight in the darkness of their bin. Now they were just brown and tired, having given up the effort. I took another bite. At least the tightly corked molasses jug had escaped the river.

Papa got to his feet and marched to the wagon, undoubtedly in search of his shot and gunpowder. Amelia cast aside her own meal, and listened to Papa's adventures with the chest just as I did. There was hope of better meals to come shining from her hungry eyes.

A drawer slammed shut and the gunpowder keg was lowered from the wagon, Papa following it. In a moment Papa had the cork out, and the keg tipped toward his powder flask. It stayed tipped for a long minute. Then Papa was lifting the entire keg, shaking it.

"Need some assistance, Papa?"

"Thank you, Phoebe. There seems to be a minor problem with the powder."

By the time I'd reached the rear of the wagon, Papa had the entire top of the keg pried off. I kneeled down next to it and stared at the black powder. It looked different. I poked it tentatively with a finger. "It's all caked up, Papa, like the flour. Will it work?"

The thunderous expression on his face gave me my answer.

"Kennan!" he roared as he stormed off to the captain's wagon. "Kennan! Have you checked your powder supply?"

That night we all ate our wilted bean sprouts without a whimper.

Everyone's wagon had been at least partially flooded in the Kansas River crossing. Thus everyone's provisions and powder were equally damaged. As we pulled up to a rare copse of trees standing next to what the guidebook claimed was the Big Vermillion Creek the next afternoon, Kennan summoned the group together.

"I'm calling a free day for tomorrow, folks. It'll give the livestock a rest, the women time to do their laundry"—he paused—"and the men time to try to dry out the gunpowder." He started to say something else, but was stopped by a high-pitched shriek from little Timothy O'Malley.

"Da! Da! What's that over there?"

Gerald O'Malley lifted his eyes to the west,

across the creek and through a gap in the trees. The rest of us followed his lead. Kennan finished his speech. "Elk. A herd of elk. And we haven't a tinker's chance of bagging any. Maybe tomorrow . . ."

Amelia and I turned away from the tempting shapes highlighted by the broad, rosy hues of the setting sun. Our stomachs thundered in sympathy.

I sighed. "Come on, Amelia, let's unyoke the oxen."

Amelia helped, but as the yoke slipped over the lead team's heads I couldn't miss the obsessive look she gave to the sturdy flanks of poor Buck and Bright.

Mama was down by the creek early the next morning, pummeling and pounding at laundry with most of the other women. Amelia, a big chunk of lye soap in one fist, was helping. I'd caught her trying to take a bite out of that same hunk of soap but a few minutes earlier, out behind the wagon when she thought no one was watching. Even I wasn't *that* hungry yet.

Papa had ordered me to collect firewood, since this grove was supposed to be the last real stand of trees for another thousand miles or so. It beat washing dirty linens. I had just selected a nice little sapling on which to test Papa's ax when I heard soft murmurings ahead. Curious, I plowed through the greenery.

The two maiden ladies, Miss Simpson and Miss Prendergast, were down on their skirted knees, inspecting a plant. At least, Miss Simpson was. Miss Prendergast had a little book open in one hand and was squinting at it nearsightedly, even though she was wearing spectacles.

"It says right here in the herbal, Emily. 'Slightly forked leaves.' Does that apply? Oh!" She'd spotted me. "Here's one of the Brown girls."

"Phoebe," I supplied.

"Phoebe. Greek for 'bright one.' Yes, I think that might apply."

"Thank you." I set down the ax. "What might you ladies be doing? Or is it polite to ask?"

Miss Prendergast stuck her finger in the book to save the page. "Quite reasonable, my dear, under the circumstances."

"We're searching for means to stave off hunger, to be quite blunt." Miss Simpson was the heartier one. She nodded toward a nearby basket heaped with greens. "Thus far we've located wild onions and garlic and a goodly amount of dandelion."

"We had no idea dandelion leaves could be consumed," Miss Prendergast added brightly. "We knew, of course, about making wine from the flowers—"

By this time I was down on my knees, too. "Would it be an imposition . . . that is . . ."

The two ladies shared a glance and apparently decided in my favor.

"The wild onion and dandelion will be the easiest to spot as you walk the oxen, my dear," offered Miss Prendergast as she removed a tiny onion from the basket. "Now study these shoots carefully. And I do believe I spotted some watercress at the far side of the creek earlier. . . ."

Those two maiden ladies were wonders. I thought about them as I wandered back and forth between the camp and the trees all morning. They were polite and dignified, like Mama, but they seemed to have a lot more grit beneath the surface.

While my pile of firewood and greens grew with my cogitations, I kept close track of the men at their own labors. They'd spread lengths of canvas on the ground beneath the sun, dumped their gunpowder upon it, and were using their wives' mortars and pestles to break up the chunks of black powder.

"Thank the Lord it's a dry day," I heard Mr. O'Malley comment as he shooed Timothy from the fascinating, dangerous material. "The black powder just naturally takes moisture to itself."

"Aye. How to get it out, that's the problem," voiced Mr. Hawkins, grinding away. "In this lifetime."

"And a short one that'll be for all of us, should we not succeed."

"Lower your voice, Gerald," boomed Captain Kennan. "Do you want the women and children abreast of all our worries?"

I stared at the men, then at the creek, its rocks and nearby bushes draped with drying linens. My gaze lingered on the creek before I ventured boldly toward the men.

"Papa?"

"Off about your business, Phoebe."

"But, Papa. Could it be possible the laundering hasn't chased off all the fish?"

Heads rose from the work.

"Never gave the water a second thought with the powder situation so pressing."

"Saints preserve us, nor did I."

"Maybe upstream, Brown?"

Papa stared past me to consider the large pile

of wood I'd already gathered. "Come here, Phoebe. Try your hand at this mortar and pestle."

I couldn't vouch for the gunpowder, but that night our family feasted on fish stuffed with watercress and onions fried in lard.

The wagons trekked on, oxen and horses hale from the rich grass that seemed to grow higher each morning. We stumbled after, more and more slowly, by Alcove Spring and the crossing of the Big Blue. We passed through the Narrows and finally reached the Platte River basin. We'd been on the road more than a month and the new vistas no longer impressed us. The whole train had grown hungry.

We paused for the nooning next to the shallow waters of the Platte—the river that would guide us and keep both our stock and ourselves in water for the next six hundred miles. It looked to be about a mile wide and an inch deep at this point, not much more than moving sand. No hope for any fish here. My attention turned to the verdant growth of the plains around us. How could there be famine with so much abundance?

The gunpowder still did not work. Twice more the men had tried to dry it out. I'd noticed Miss

Simpson watching their third effort. She stood staunchly, black hair efficiently pulled into a no-nonsense bun, hands on hips, obviously fighting back a thought. She lost the struggle.

"Gentlemen," she finally said.

A few men raised their eyes questioningly. Miss Simpson had never interfered before.

"Gentlemen," she continued. "According to my calculations, effective gunpowder is seventy-five percent saltpeter, ten percent sulphur, and fifteen percent charcoal. But the mix must be *precise*. Could it be possible that your current substance has separated, like cream to the top of milk? If so, it might be nearly impossible to regain the correct combination. . . ." Frowns and grimaces being her only response, she stopped.

The men bent over their labors again. Afterward, they loaded their guns with hope. The tests fizzled, with one notable exception. The spinsters' drover—a man of few words, and those unfit for most ears—primed and cocked his rifle. As he was lowest in the male pecking order, he patiently waited while the other men's experiments failed. His turn coming at last, he pulled his trigger with a grunt.

"Je-hosephat!"

Stars exploded along with the drover's exclamation as his gun backfired. I moved off fast, along with the rest of the watchers. Happy Hawkins rushed for her medical supplies. The drover sank to the ground and began picking shot from his pockmarked face.

Captain Kennan set down his own weapon and pulled at his moustache. "Well, I guess the mixture of the powder's all wrong now."

Miss Simpson merely twitched her formidable nose at this backhanded tribute. The experiments, however, were discontinued.

After the drover incident, the men set traps of every contrivance around the camp each night. Occasionally a rabbit or groundhog was caught, and once, a coyote. It grew harder to find succulent greens, as everyone was now searching for them. Even Mama had forsaken her hard, splintery seat to join the hunt. She was particularly effective at robbing birds' nests.

"It's all in the proper experience, Phoebe," she explained to me when I asked how in thunder she'd come up with nearly a dozen of the tiny eggs one afternoon. "After all those years tending hens, a woman just *knows* where the eggs are likely to be tucked."

"I never would have thought keeping fowl could be so useful, Mama."

Mama handed me some of her bounty. "Be careful not to crack them before they get to the bowl, Phoebe. Our journey thus far has made a few truths more obvious to me. A woman must learn to be resourceful. She must learn to use whatever experiences come her way. It's our best defense, daughter."

Mama drew the line at rattlesnakes, though. Others didn't. They were chased, cudgeled, roasted, and consumed with relish. Something had to be done. When the men saw those first buffalo, they decided to do it.

It was the third day along the Platte, and buffalo hadn't really been expected for another week or two. Captain Kennan had left the nooning early on his horse, to scout ahead. He came galloping back as we swilled molasses-laced coffee for our dinner.

"Buffalo!" he bellowed. "Buffalo! Not more than two miles to the west!"

The entire camp gathered around his heaving, frothing horse.

"*Real* buffalo?"

"They as big as we hoped?"

"How we gonna get 'em, Kennan?"

Kennan swayed off the horse to address the most pertinent question. "We'll get 'em like the Injuns do. There's a bluff nearby, with a drop. We stampede them over the edge. We should be able to shout up enough noise for that."

I watched Papa scratch his head. His hair had begun thinning out in the last week or two. And his neck didn't seem as thick. He glanced at the other men. "Anything's worth a try. Another day or two and we'd have to start butchering our livestock."

"Brown's right," Hawkins added. "Weaken our teams like that, we'll never make the Territory."

Decided, the men ran for their mounts. Captain Kennan tarried to gulp a big ladleful of water from Sarah. "Many thanks, daughter." He turned to the rest of us. "You women know how to do it. Move the wagons on up another mile or so, then set up camp. We won't have so far to haul the carcasses!" A last thought made him pause. "Set up those meat-drying racks we made from the guidebook's directions. Size of that herd, there'll be a couple tons of buffalo to preserve."

As every man in camp galloped off, Amelia stood next to me, whispering dreamily. "Meat. *Steaks*. Big, juicy steaks dripping over the fire. Soup. Ribs. Liver. . . ."

The juices were already running in my own mouth.

"Enough, Amelia. Never count your buffalo till they're bagged."

THREE

*W*e women and children walked with more enthusiasm and lighter hearts than we had in days. Even Miss Simpson and Miss Prendergast were prodding oxen with the best of us—Miss Simpson her own wagon, and Miss Prendergast that of Zachary Judd, the bachelor blacksmith in whom she'd recently taken a neighborly interest.

We did everything that was expected of us. We stopped and set up camp within the suggested mile. We started fires for the meat. And we waited.

In the distance was only a thick haze of dust. I watched the dust begin to settle. There should have been more activity.

I took my concerns to Mama and Amelia, who were burning our hard-won collection of dried buffalo chips with a passion that bordered on extravagance. Firewood had been only a distant memory for more than a week.

"There won't be any chips left for the meat, Mama, when it comes."

She glanced up. "Your father ordered us to be ready, Phoebe, and I intend to please him. A happy man is a less truculent one."

"Has it ever occurred to you, Mama, that a good piece of our energies goes into keeping Papa happy?"

Mama paused, another chip halfway to the fire. "It may seem so at times, child. . . . Heaven knows there are moments when I—"

"When what?"

"Nothing." She tossed the chip into the flames. "How else are we to proceed?"

Amelia looked like she might have an answer for that one, but chose to keep her mouth shut. I rubbed the ribs beginning to stick out beneath the cotton of my dress and changed the subject. "Do you think, perhaps, the men have been longer at the hunt than they ought?"

Mama poked at her fire with unexpected passion. "You should have learned, daughter, that men also have their own standards for time."

"You're probably right, Mama, but I'm walking out there anyhow. Maybe they could use an extra hand."

Amelia rose from the fire. "There's nothing left to do here. I'll keep you company. Four eyes are better than two for spotting rattlesnakes."

"With buffalo in the offing you want to catch more rattlesnakes, Amelia?"

Amelia shuddered. "Certainly not! I never want to lay eyes on another of the slithery, slimy, treacherous creatures! As for their insidious ticking—" She stiffened. "What's that sound?"

"La-di-da, Amelia. It's only our new bracelets."

Hannah and Sarah Kennan, who'd quietly crept up, jingled the rattles around their wrists evocatively. Apparently the twins had chosen to join us. So had Lizzie and Margaret O'Malley. We all set off toward the haze in the distance. It was just as well, because when we arrived Amelia and I couldn't have handled the situation on our own.

There wasn't a single buffalo in sight, but the prairie grass was stomped flat as far as we could see, right to the edge of the bluff Captain Kennan had mentioned. More frightening were the horses nonchalantly cropping clumps of that leftover grass, reins flopping over their heads, saddles empty.

Hannah screamed first. "Something's happened!"

Sarah swooned, plop onto a pile of fresh buffalo chips.

I didn't wait for the rest of the hysterics. I

picked up my skirts and ran to the edge of the bluff.

It was only a forty-foot drop, but apparently that was enough. The men had been successful. There were half a dozen buffalo twitching on the ground below. There were wicked-looking vultures standing off, in wait.

And there were our men.

"Amelia!" I roared. "Amelia! We've got to get down the bluff!"

The easy way would've been to run around it. But that might take too long. I lowered myself over the edge, grabbed for roots and footholds, and started bellying down. To her credit, Amelia followed.

Halting partway, I shouted back to the O'Malleys above. "Ride one of those horses back to camp for help. Quickly! It's getting dark!"

I found Papa unconscious, with his legs pinned beneath a huge bull. Amelia shoved and I pulled. On the last pull that freed him, Papa screeched.

"Thank the Lord. He's alive. Come on, Amelia, there's ten more to account for."

Amelia didn't move. Now that Papa was saved she just stood there, eyes registering the carnage around us, tears streaming down her face. It was hard to be the practical one, hard to force myself away from the anguish that could come too easily, overpowering me just like my quilt had at cold winter milking time. I rubbed at the pounding in my head before gently shaking Amelia's arm.

"Help me, Amelia. Please. There might be another life we could save."

Mr. Hawkins was breathing, but not otherwise moving. The drover had gone on to his reward. So had Captain Kennan and all the other men. Except for Mr. O'Malley and Zachary Judd, the bachelor. They were moaning and twitching like the buffalo. There didn't seem much we could do for the survivors aside from trying to make them as comfortable as possible, and wrapping both our petticoats around a bloody wound in Mr. O'Malley's side.

Amelia and I were sitting in the dark, holding Papa's hands and watching the moon rise when the women, torches in hand, came in procession around the bluff.

I never want to live through anything like that night again. The sun was rising when we had a trench dug big enough for the burial. We all stood around and said the Lord's Prayer and sang "Rock of Ages." Badly. It was hard to get up much enthusiasm for it. The weeping and keening were too distracting.

Yet in the strained moments that followed, thinking more on the words of that old hymn began to help in a curious way. Most of the women present, they were hoping that Rock would cleft open then and there and swallow them up, too. We'd all followed the men this far, and now the men were either gone or useless. It would have been nice to hide in the Lord . . . but the sun began to shine brighter and hotter. It outlined the vast emptiness of the prairie surrounding us—making it apparent that the Lord helps those who help themselves. And if we women and children didn't start helping ourselves soon, we might as well just dig another trench and crawl into it.

It was Miss Simpson who began to pull us together at last.

"Ladies." She held up an arm after the last clod of earth had been patted down. "Ladies. And young ladies and Master Timothy O'Malley. Are we to waste the parting gift of these men?" She waved toward the buffalo strewn around us. "No! Hunger still sits upon us, weakening us. We must take this gift and use it for our strength. With that strength we will be able to make decisions!"

More persuasive than Captain Kennan in his prime, Miss Simpson ran through a list of simple directives, alternately chivvying or bullying all those blank-faced women. She must have been a schoolteacher in her former life. Or maybe even a headmistress, she was that commanding. We captured the horses and prepared pallets. Survivors and meat both were ferried back to camp.

Three days passed in grieving and the smoking and drying of buffalo meat. By the third day the surviving men had recovered enough to tell us what had happened. All except for Mr. Hawkins, who was fine everywhere but in his mind. He just wandered around, lost and useless, with Mrs. Hawkins shaking her head as she tried to catch him and spoonfeed him a meal. Mr. O'Malley suffered from a bad gash in his side and was forced to lie as still as possible after Mrs. Hawkins stitched him up. Zachary Judd had a broken hipbone that Miss Prendergast fussed over. As for Papa, both legs were fractured. We'd set and wrapped them, and suffering or not, he soon proved there wasn't anything wrong with his tongue.

"Move that left leg an inch, Ruth. And scratch the toe. It itches."

"Yes, Henry."

"*Ahhh*. . . . Hand me Kennan's jug, Phoebe."

"Yes, Papa."

Papa took a long medicinal swallow for the pain. It turned out that Captain Kennan had had a number of jugs privately hoarded in his wagon. His wife had passed them out to the wounded for succor.

"We snuck up on the herd quietly," Papa started. "Just like Kennan told us. On his signal we were to whoop up a storm. We did. The beasts got confused and stampeded, just as they were meant to. . . . Unfortunately, the horses got even more confused. Instead of holding to the perimeter of the herd, we were sucked into it. It seemed like there were thousands of those great beasts, milling about." Papa sighed. "After that, we somehow got separated from our horses, and the edge of the bluff just crept up on us, I guess."

Amelia had been hovering near the fire. "Have another buffalo rib, Papa."

Papa straightened his back into the wagon wheel we'd propped him against. "I might as well."

On the third evening the women began gathering together around neutral territory—a wagon not grieving over lost or wounded husbands. That territory happened to be the wagon of Miss Simpson and Miss Prendergast. They'd lost their drover, true, but as Mrs. Hawkins put it, "Those two hadn't any tears or years invested in *him*."

Papa—still propped up against the wagon—was not pleased at the desertion. "Where are you all going, Ruth?"

"To a meeting, Henry."

"How do you know how to hold a meeting? The only meetings you've ever attended were for quilting, or organizing flowers for the church back home."

"It's high time I learned how, then, isn't it, Henry?"

"Who's going to scratch my toes?"

Mama handed him the whip. "This should reach, Henry."

When we joined the crowd we all mingled, sharing more general condolences. We weren't quite sure what to do next. It was Happy Hawkins who finally gathered her skirts together and pulled herself up the wagon traces to the seat, so we could all see and hear her.

"Friends," she started in. "Friends, we got ourselves a situation. Which direction do we go next?

Back home in defeat to what kith and kin we left behind, or farther on west? We got meat enough to take us to China, but not a single useful man left in the party—"

Maybe that was the wrong approach, because handkerchiefs started coming out again, and Sarah and Mrs. Kennan both began serious swooning sways. Mama raised her hand timidly.

"What is it, Ruth?"

"It seems to me, Happy—"

"Speak up!"

Mama raised her voice. "Well, it seems to me that more important than deciding if we're to go back, or forward, or even stay right here"—her voice faltered, then strengthened—"even more important, ladies, is coming to understand that for the first time in our lives we've got to rely entirely on our own resourcefulness . . . to *take charge* of our own destinies."

Amelia and I shared a disbelieving look. Mama was saying *this*? Our sweet, subservient Mama?

Mrs. Hawkins motioned Mama to the front of the crowd and up to the seat beside her. Mama's voice continued clear as a bell when she faced us. "And it is not just the decision of what to make for dinner, or what vegetables to plant in the garden, or what pattern to sew into a quilt!" The last came out triumphantly as Mama's tiny body seemed to stretch about three feet.

"Amelia," I hissed. "Amelia! Has Mama been reading those Lowell slavery tracts of yours?"

"Heaven forbid!" She stopped, eyes narrowed. "How did you know about them, Phoebe Brown?"

Lizzie O'Malley shushed us, nudging us expectantly toward Mama in the front.

"I know what's going through your minds," Mama continued. "Wait until we're stronger to make a decision. But when shall we be stronger? When the numbness of our grief has worn off? Next week? . . . Next year?" Mama gulped for a breath, then finished. "I say we have the strength in us now. I say we've always had this hidden strength. The strength to be responsible for ourselves!"

Mama had said her piece. She stepped down, and so did Mrs. Hawkins, as Miss Simpson replaced them on the wagon seat.

"Ladies! Mrs. Brown has hit upon the very meat of the issue. Without men in charge, *we* must take over the reins of this party, both physically and metaphorically. Now is the time to search deep into our hearts and souls." She paused a moment to allow the searching to proceed.

Some of those quiet new widows, especially the two gray-haired ones, Mrs. Davis and Mrs. Russell—who hadn't uttered a peep the entire journey—stared back out of confused faces.

Miss Simpson helped them along. "You *know* we are capable of doing it!" She waited, eyes afire, for recognition to register. It was starting to simmer up nicely.

"The only question remaining is this. Shall we make for the promised land of Oregon—where society is not as rigid, where new things may be possible for our gender—or shall we return to the constraints of the East?"

For myself, I hadn't been that anxious to leave the East in the first place. But having gotten this far, I figured Miss Simpson had a point. There wasn't much worse that could happen to us. And growing up to be allowed to make a few decisions—like Papa always had—held a certain appeal.

From the expressions on their faces, a goodly number of the other females were thinking the same. Especially the younger, childless widows like willow-slim Mrs. Vernon, or that curly-haired Kincaid woman. Even Mabel Hatch, wed only four months back in St. Louis. They were probably thinking it more in terms of Mama's thoughts, though, than Miss Simpson's. Spending years of your life being allowed to decide only the contents of dinner—if one were fortunate, because I knew for a fact that Papa had a controlling interest on that subject more often than not—ground a person down.

"This land around us is so big," whimpered Mabel Hatch.

"Lord, and the Oregon Country so much bigger." That was Mrs. O'Malley.

"Maybe its bigness can hold bigger ideas, too." Miss Prendergast's eyes sparkled behind her spectacles.

"Ideas about women being capable of more than just cooking . . . and laundry and needlework?" Mrs. Kincaid's words came out tentatively.

"The men did so want to get to the New Land," Mrs. Davis burst out at last. "Our success would be a fitting tribute, better than tombstones."

"But it's going to be even wilder out there," sniffled Tabitha Kennan. "And I always wanted my girls raised civilized. Among gentility. George never did understand. And now he's deserted us completely without a single last directive—"

"It wasn't *his* fault." Hannah propped up her wilting mother.

"Maybe it was his fault in a sense," Mama opined. "All the men's faults for forcing us to uproot our old lives. But now that those roots are almost free, can't we learn to set them down again in a new way? In a new place?"

"Amen!" yelled Happy Hawkins.

Mabel Hatch opened her mouth as if to offer further resistance, but Miss Simpson was taking no chances. "Well, ladies?" she prodded. "What will it be?"

"Oregon!" I shouted.

Next to me, Amelia straightened, strong and lithe in the final rays of the setting sun. "Oregon!" she seconded.

Others joined in, and soon we women were standing tall—especially Mama.

"We can do it!"

"Let's roll west at first light!"

Come sunrise the next morning, Mama made up a nest of quilts and feather beds in the center of the wagon and Amelia and I hoisted Papa into it. The exuberance of the previous night was already beginning to wear off. Papa was not taking his enforced rest well, was not readily handing over the reins of control to his women.

"Ouch! Watch those legs, daughters! Confound this narrowness. Feels like I'm being banished to a cave. . . . Have the animals been watered?"

"Yes, Papa," I sighed.

His elbows poked the pillow into a more comfortable position. "Did they drink enough? Enough to get them to the nooning?"

"When an ox wants to drink, Papa, he'll drink. When he doesn't—"

"You lead it back into the Platte and convince it, Phoebe."

"Yes, Papa."

"Did you grease the axles like I ordered? The prairie's getting dry—"

He would've gone on like that the entire blessed morning. Amelia and I glanced at each other over his reclining body. Of one mind, we snaked out of the wagon without another "Yes, Papa."

The problems of the road were simpler. We jockeyed our wagons into line and no one complained when Tabitha Kennan handed Miss Simpson her husband's guidebook. Miss Simpson accepted it gracefully and waved it for all to see.

"I'm not taking over Captain Kennan's role as leader, ladies. Happy Hawkins would be far more competent at that than I—had she not an invalid to care for. But I will be available for guidance and support. I've had my own guidebook these many days, and I know the next six hundred miles along the Platte should be the easiest. Midway along the river, we'll have the comfort of Fort Laramie, and fresh supplies—gunpowder being our priority item. If we can make it to Laramie, we can make it to Oregon. Until then, there's enough meat to keep all of us strong.

"In the meantime, for everyone's comfort, might I suggest that we rotate wagons each day? Last at evening, first at morning. Miss Prendergast and I have already noted the deleterious effects of dust at the tail end of the train, having spent the entire past week journeying in that very position. None of us need suffer unnecessarily." She inspected us. "If you approve, give me a show of hands."

Miss Simpson received her support. She really was taking over. Everyone knew it. No one minded. In the coolness of a new day, learning to be strong, to be a leader, took some getting used to. It was enough for the moment to have someone to follow, someone to guide us away from that trench of graves.

Regular meals of fresh meat strengthened us, and the anticipated solace of Fort Laramie ahead gave us hope. Even better than hope, it gave us a point to focus on. Miss Simpson had said in no uncertain terms that if we could make it to

Laramie, we could make it to Oregon. We all chose to believe her. Fate and the buffalo having relieved us of our working men, it was necessary to believe in someone.

The trail along the Platte went smoothly for a few days. It slowly occurred to me that little had really changed since the disaster and that one heady moment of beginning to grasp at the reins of control. We females continued with the work we'd always done, while shouldering the extra responsibilities imposed upon us. Responsibilities such as safely pasturing the animals each night, scouting the trail ahead, greasing those groaning axles. There were just fewer orders, as there were fewer men. Papa kept trying, though.

"Phoebe!" he'd yell through the canvas. "Are those beasts yoked up right? They're pulling unevenly."

"The ground is uneven, Papa," I'd shout back.

"Amelia! Our horse is tangled on his lead."

"I'll fix it directly, Papa."

"Ruth? I can't smell the river. Is that *woman* leading us away from the river?"

"*Miss Simpson* is doing her Christian best, Henry," Mama would point out from her perch. "And you'd do *your* Christian best by thanking God for your deliverance, instead of badgering one and all."

Papa would lapse into silence. But only for a few blessed minutes.

Margaret O'Malley confessed that her family was traveling under a similar burden when we met at the Platte to water horses a few nights later.

"God forgive me, Phoebe, but sometimes I wish it was Da's tongue that had been gored, and not his side. Ma has her hands full with the young ones, as always, and it's Lizzie and I must bear the brunt of it."

I considered her words as Papa's horse took a leisurely drink between the guzzling oxen. "If we're doing the work, Margaret—you and Lizzie and Amelia and I—maybe it's time we stopped acting like children."

"Whatever do you mean, Phoebe?"

"If we drop everything and keep running every time they order us around . . ."

My words hovered between us.

"Disobey Da? He'd have his belt onto me in a minute."

"He can't move, Margaret."

Margaret's blue eyes widened at the new concept and her freckles took on an even stronger definition.

"And not exactly disobey," I added. "Just develop—"

"Develop what?"

"—A deaf ear, Margaret."

Margaret crossed herself. "You'll be a bad influence, Phoebe Brown. Still, it would be so peaceful . . ."

"Come along, Blackie." I led the horse to pasture with a grin. No one had ever called me a bad influence before.

It was a day short of June, but it was hot when we arrived a few afternoons later at Cottonwood Springs. It was adjacent to the Platte, a small spring-fed pond surrounded by a few cottonwoods already gray with dust. The livestock had been cared for, Mama was starting the supper, and Amelia and I were down by the pool with the Kennan twins. High-topped boots and stockings off and skirts shifted well above our knees, we were blissfully soaking our feet and squeezing wet handkerchiefs over our faces.

"Daddy would never have allowed this," Hannah said, with a small snuffle of remembrance. " 'An unseemly exhibition,' he'd call it."

"It's his feet that would be soaking," Sarah added. "Poor dear. He'll never see us with husbands."

"I'm sure he's looking down from heaven now"—Amelia was trying to be considerate—"and will be on your wedding day."

Hannah jerked her feet out of the pool and hid her knees. "I hope not. At least not this instant!"

Hannah need not have worried about her father. It was other eyes that were watching the four of us with interest. Eyes connected to heads that sprouted feathers. I caught the movement first, through the waist-high grasses surrounding the far side of the pool.

"Indians!" I gasped. "Wild Indians!"

FOUR

$\mathscr{I}$ t was my first sight of *real* Indians. Not tame Indians like back in Independence. All of us—four girls on one side of the spring, Indians on the other—froze. Heartbeats suspended, we stared at each other under the hot blue sky.

Surprisingly, it was Sarah who broke the spell—Sarah, the twin taken to swooning at the drop of a hat. Calmly, and with admirable aplomb, she covered her exposed knees. "My Lord," she breathed, "but ain't they *handsome!*"

As if on cue, the Indians—only two as it turned out—rose from the grass and bolted. In that one moment of full sight, however, it appeared Sarah was correct. Both braves were in the prime of young manhood. Their high cheekbones and strong noses set off bronzed faces free of ornamentation. Their bronzed, hairless chests were equally bare and splendidly muscled. But their heads were dressed with extraordinary feathers, and one of them sported a necklace of claws. They disappeared too fast for me to inspect the decorations on their buckskin trousers, but *colorful* was the word that came to mind.

Gradually, I pulled my legs from the water as Amelia followed suit. "Well," I thought aloud, "I suppose we ought to tell someone about this."

"Not Papa," Amelia stated.

"No, definitely not Papa."

Sarah and Hannah's mouths were still agape. Amelia and I had to haul them back to camp.

Miss Simpson dealt with the incident quickly and practically.

"It had to happen sooner or later. We are going through Indian lands now, after all. Probably Pawnee. According to my studies the Platte would be bordering on their territory. They're considered nonhostile." She continued her earlier inquisition of the four of us. "Did you notice any weapons? Rifles? Bows and arrows?"

We shook our heads dumbly. The entire affair had only lasted a few seconds, even if it had seemed an eternity. And we'd been staring at the young braves themselves, not searching for accoutrements.

"Very well." Miss Simpson nodded. "We'll begin sentry duty tonight. It's too late to get the wagons in a circle, so we'll start that tomorrow."

"But our guns, Miss Simpson—"

"*We* know our guns don't work, Phoebe. The Indians don't. Besides, it's not a war we're looking to start, is it?"

Miss Simpson set up a revolving sentry roster beginning with the oldest women. They would work in pairs, alternating three-hour shifts throughout the night. That was going to use up our woman-power fairly fast. Amelia and I and the other older girls figured it wouldn't be long before our turns came around.

Nothing happened that first night, nor the second, either. When the surprise came, it was in broad daylight on the third day beyond Cottonwood Springs.

We'd paused early for the nooning to freshen up our water at Fremont Springs. I was topping off the level in a leathern bag that usually hung by the side of the wagon, thinking about the spring's namesake—John C. Frémont, the Hero of the West, the Pathfinder who'd explored this very trail only a few years back. . . . Of a sudden, a funny, prickly feeling ran down my spine. I swiped at my back, but it wasn't the usual perspiration. That tingle hovered there, like a viper fixing on the perfect spot to set his fangs. Finally I turned my eyes to a low bluff just south of the Platte. And there they were, rising over the bluff on ponies. Practically a whole tribe of Indians.

I opened my mouth to shout a warning, but there wasn't any need. Seemed like the entire camp was suffering from that same prickly feeling—and now we were all staring at the row of ponies silhouetted against the sky.

"It's them, Hannah!" Sarah began whooping down the whole line of wagons at her sister.

"Hush up at once, Sarah Kennan! I'll deal with this." Miss Simpson strode forward, waving the rest of us to silence and submission. Happy Hawkins paused long enough to root through her wagon for a useless weapon before trailing after our leader.

Since there wasn't much else to be done, I lugged the water bag back to our wagon and stood, counting Indians. There were ten of them, enough to have taken us easily, had they but known. The two braves from Cottonwood Springs were in the lead, followed by half a dozen other young men. The group was rounded out by several venerable-looking elders. They all carried rifles, slung easy by their sides—simple to get at, but not necessarily signi-fying belligerence, I hoped. I was focusing on the stripes freshly painted on their chests, wondering what they meant, when I heard a plaintive voice from inside the wagon. I'd entirely forgotten about Papa.

"Ruth! Amelia! . . . Phoebe? What in tarnation's going on out there?"

"Nothing, Papa," I answered. "Just a few Pawnee come to visit. Miss Simpson's dealing with them."

"Indians! Are they armed?"

"Calm down, Papa. Of course they're armed. Ever heard of an unarmed Indian?"

I could hear him struggling vainly within his cocoon of bedclothes. "Blast! I can't move an inch! When will I be free of these restraints?"

"Maybe by Oregon, Papa." Surely the healing would take that long. "We wouldn't want to mess up your legs beforetimes. . . . Sorry, I've got to go."

"Phoebe, come back here!"

"Presently, Papa."

Miss Simpson and the Pawnee were parting ways, the Indians drifting slowly back to the rise and down its far slope. What had she said to them? What had they wanted? I found out soon enough.

"Hannah and Sarah Kennan!" Miss Simpson bellowed.

The twins came forward reluctantly. So did everyone else, with no reluctance whatsoever. All those damp-faced widows crowded around, eyes newly bright with speculation.

"Hannah and Sarah, did you tell me the entire truth about that episode by Cottonwood Springs the other day?"

Mrs. Kennan bustled closer to put an arm around each daughter. "Emily Simpson, I'll thank you not to speak in such a tone to my little girls—"

"No insult intended, Tabitha, but if you'll only look upon your offspring with an open mind you'll notice they're no longer little girls." Miss Simpson's voice turned dry. "Our visitors certainly noticed. Particularly two young men known as Panther Claw and Wind Pony."

"Was Panther the one with the claws around his neck?" Sarah blurted out eagerly.

"And Wind the one with horses galloping across his britches?" Hannah asked.

Mrs. Kennan dropped her protective arms to glare at her daughters, while Miss Simpson shook her head at the twins' responses. "Undoubtedly yes to each. For a wonder they spoke a little English. Probably picked it up from mountain men passing through to Rendezvous—"

"But what did they want, Miss Simpson?"

Happy Hawkins answered the girls. "You. They wanted to barter for your hands in marriage. Said

they'd never seen anything like to your golden hair."
She sniffed. "Nearly turned poetic, they did."

This caught Amelia's attention. "What exactly
did they offer for Hannah and Sarah? And how did
they phrase it?"

Miss Simpson took over with a snort. "They
claimed each had a whole string of ponies they'd
been saving up for brides. They offered ten apiece.
When I said that was outright ridiculous, they
upped the offer to twelve without blinking an eye."

Hannah was dazzled by that information, but
Sarah began acting as if she was fixing to float off
into one of her swoons. Did she consider the price
too low, or was it Miss Simpson's refusal that was
upsetting her? Hannah put out an arm to support
her sister. "Did they say anything else?"

"Only that the sun would never rise again for
either of them until the Great Spirit had united the
four of you together. I told them you were too
young for marriage and they'd better get used to a
lot of gray days."

"Oh, sister, my heart—" Sarah proceeded to
well and truly faint. Amelia and I helped Hannah
catch her while the twins' mother trotted off for a
ladle of water.

Miss Simpson just shook her head again.
"We've wasted enough time on this nonsense. Get

these wagons rolling. Only another two hundred miles and we'll be safely in Fort Laramie and out of Pawnee country."

"I don't believe Miss Simpson was *ever* in love."

Sarah Kennan's lament floated all down the line of young ladies soaking their sore toes in the Platte before bedtime. Lizzie O'Malley, seventeen just like Amelia was, touched her fiery hair. "Saints be praised they didn't spy *me* first. I'd just die if I were pursued by a *heathen*—"

"They did mention the Great Spirit, Lizzie," Amelia reminded her. "I believe that's what Indians call God. So they're not precisely *heathens*—"

"Don't be playing with words that way, Amelia. Sure and you know very well what I'm referring to. Heaven knows how they live, or what they eat—" she stopped to squint farther down the river through the red rays of the setting sun. "Maureen O'Malley! You drag Timothy out of those currents this minute. And Mary Rose, too. You know they can't swim!" Her hand reached up for her hair again. "Anyway, it's my head that'll be hidden in a scarf *and* bonnet at the first sign of any more visitors like those Pawnee today."

"Me, too!" Margaret fervently agreed.

Hannah snorted, almost with the authority of Miss Simpson. "You've nothing to worry about yet, Margaret O'Malley." Her attention turned to me. "Nor you, Phoebe."

That smarted a little. Even if I had no interest in wedded bliss with a Pawnee—or any other male, for that matter—I didn't care for being thought of as a child. The long weeks on the trail seemed to have started something sprouting in my chest area, after all. "Just because Margaret and I aren't as advanced as the rest of you—"

Hannah let out her yellow braids dreamily and talked right over me, as if I weren't even there. "I'd live anywhere with Wind. In a tent, under the stars . . . never in my life have I laid eyes on a more exciting young man."

"Except for Panther, sister," Sarah interrupted. "There does seem to be a family resemblance. Do you suppose they're brothers?"

"Maybe cousins, Sarah. And it wasn't fair of Miss Simpson to send them off without even consulting us or Mother."

"I can't exactly say that Mother would approve of such an alliance, sister. And poor Daddy would surely turn over in his grave. However, I truly cannot see how that would further incapacitate Daddy at this point—"

Hannah continued her twin's thoughts. "Mother might be persuaded if we only begged long and hard enough."

"Mother does have difficulty in denying us our desires," Sarah concluded with a smirk.

Lizzie crossed herself. "Thank the good Lord for Miss Simpson. Someone has to have some sense around here, for you two surely don't. Unwashed Pawnee. *Ugh.* I suppose you would have run off with Esquimaux just as readily."

"What's an Esquimau?"

"Never mind, Hannah. Lizzie is just jealous they didn't pick her." Sarah tossed her hair, now loose to her waist, like her sister's. It caught the last glints of the dying sun before the prairie turned dark.

Lizzie got up, reaching for her boots. "Timothy! Girls! It's bedtime!"

With yawns, we all straggled back to our wagons.

Panther Claw and Wind Pony turned up again the next afternoon. They followed parallel to our train at a decent distance, pacing us. Aside from the two strings of ponies trailing behind them, they were by themselves.

There was plenty of time to tally those horses as the afternoon wore on. Fourteen in each string. I had to hand it to those two braves. They'd upped the marriage price. Sympathy for the young men grew within me. Fourteen horses must have been an enormous investment. They were truly smitten.

At the first sign of the Pawnee's approach, Miss Simpson had ordered the twins into their wagon. As the afternoon wore on, however, their mother grew weary of leading the oxen. She was unused to the job her daughters usually performed, and the Kennan wagon dropped farther and farther back in the line. When it slid into position just in front of our wagon—the last one that day—I watched Sarah and Hannah hanging from the rear opening of the whitetop, craning their necks for a sight of the braves. Finally, they jumped down. Making sure neither their mother nor Miss Simpson was watching, they both raised an arm toward the Indians, as if to wave.

"Hannah. Sarah." It was Amelia, walking on the far side of our oxen. "Even Pawnee might consider that forward."

Arms were dropped with scowls.

"Oh, pooh, Amelia." Hannah pouted. "How are Wind Pony and Panther to know we're interested?"

"They may be taken with your hair, Hannah, but according to books I've read on the subject—"

"What books?" Sarah asked.

"Certain novels by James Fenimore Cooper, who seems to have some expertise—"

"Where'd you get them, Amelia?" I was curious. "We didn't have copies back in Massachusetts."

"Lowell had a lending library, Phoebe. Anyway, according to Mr. Cooper, Indians prefer their women silent and submissive."

"That doesn't sound any different from Papa or any other white male I've ever known, Amelia."

"Precisely, Phoebe. Perhaps our races are not all that different, after all."

"Hannah and Sarah Kennan! Get straight back into that wagon. This minute!"

Miss Simpson had snuck up on us, a threatening whip in hand. She must have been a headmistress, indeed. Maybe even a jailer. Certainly she put up with no nonsense. The twins crept back into the lumbering whitetop.

Directly after we had closed ranks in a tight circle of wagons at our evening stopover, the Pawnee approached. Miss Simpson and Happy Hawkins were once more the designated spokesmen. This time, though, Mrs. Kennan was invited to join the negotiations—so long as she kept "calm, collected, and quiet," as Miss Simpson phrased it.

The meeting was conducted just outside the circle. Naturally, the first thing we girls did was crawl underneath those wagons and peek out through the wheel spokes. Amelia and I were wedged on either side of Hannah and Sarah, just in case they needed poking or restraining. The twins were in such a dither it may have made more sense to gag and fetter them, but Amelia and I were giving them the benefit of the doubt.

Panther and Wind staked their horses and walked over solemnly, almost ceremoniously. For the first time I got to inspect them properly. They were all decked out for the occasion. Both braves had smoothly shaven skulls on either side of a thick ridge of black hair that snaked from the center of their foreheads to the nape of their necks. Sticking straight up out of these scalp locks were wondrous, exotic colored feathers arranged in neat rows.

The braves' faces had dabs of paint on them today, and—wonder of wonders—there were beaded earrings hanging from their lobes! Not only that, but even in the heat they'd taken a care to sling fancy fur blankets across one shoulder each, just partially covering their naked chests.

I guess I could have laid there and stared all day and all night, too, only the discussion began and I had to concentrate on catching every word. Panther spoke up first. Next to me, Sarah moaned. I was afraid she might drift off into insensibility again just at the sound of his voice. It did have a nice, rich timbre. I gave Sarah a good pinch to be safe. She jerked her head toward me in protest, cracking it on the wagon spokes. I ignored the sudden venom in her eyes.

"O Great and Wise Mother of Wagons of Women," Panther started out. That was obviously directed at Miss Simpson. She'd appreciate the "Great and Wise" part all right, but if wagering weren't considered uncouth and unfeminine I'd wager the compliment still wouldn't melt butter in her mouth.

"O Great and Wise Mother," Panther repeated slowly, working each word carefully through his head. Then he cast his eyes down, obviously searching for the rest of his memorized speech. He found, instead, Sarah's eyes staring up at him in adulation. I could practically hear the click as the glances locked on to each other.

Wind Pony was prodding his friend now, to no avail. Wind swallowed and took over manfully. "Ten horses not enough. Twelve horses not enough."

Wind Pony believed in getting down to business.

"For golden brides, bring *fourteen* horses." He held up ten fingers, then another four, to make sure we were all working with the same arithmetic. "*Each.*" To further prove his veracity, Wind turned to motion at the ponies grazing peacefully just beyond. "Is all," he continued. "No more. Many moons we fight and raid to get."

He stood even taller at these words, proud of his prowess and accomplishments. I heard a squeak from Hannah over by the next wheel and out of the corner of my eye caught Amelia thrusting her hand over the twin's mouth. Wind Pony spread his arms beseechingly.

"Wind Pony and Panther Claw become great braves. Provide well for squaws."

It was now Miss Simpson's turn. I could only see her back, but I recognized the iron in it.

"Your offers are honorable. We thank you for making them in good faith. We thank you for the honor of choosing Hannah and Sarah—"

Miss Simpson stopped. She must've known she'd made a mistake as soon as the names slipped from her mouth. Wind Pony perked right up, and Panther Claw wrenched his eyes from Sarah's. You could almost see the young men playing the names over in their heads.

"Nevertheless," Miss Simpson plowed on, "nevertheless, these young ladies are still too young for such a commitment."

"Com-mit-e-ment?" Panther queried.

"They cannot marry you!" snapped Miss Simpson. "They do not have enough moons!"

"Look like plenty enough moons to Wind Pony!"

"Young man, you are impertinent!"

Neither inquired after the meaning of that word. It was perfectly obvious.

"You no take horses?"

"We no take horses. You no take girls."

The two braves raised a hand each and backed off. Panther nudged Wind and gestured toward our wagon. Even restrained by Amelia, Hannah had managed to free a hand and waved madly through the spokes. A ghost of a smile crossed Wind's face before he turned to Panther and their wedding gifts and rode off.

The thumping started over my head before I could pull myself out from under the wagon. *My* wagon, I suddenly realized. "Yes, Papa?"

"What in thunder's going on out there? Nobody tells me anything anymore. I could just expire and go off to heaven like the other men, and it wouldn't even be noticed!"

Papa was feeling sorry for himself again.

"Nothing, Papa. Just another marriage offer. You certainly were right about young ladies being in demand out west."

FIVE

$\mathcal{I}$t was more than a hundred endless miles closer to Laramie and a good week later before we were to learn those two young Pawnee had just as much iron in them as Miss Simpson. But I'll work up to that in good time. Meanwhile the whole train kept prodding oxen, walking the leather off boot soles in a universal desire to accomplish the first piece of our goal. We also kept trying to put up with the Kennan twins—a task equally challenging.

Hannah and Sarah played at being desolate and impossible by turns. In between castigating Miss Simpson's hard heart and their mother's sudden, unnatural intransigence on the subject of marriage, the twins brooded over whether they'd ever see the Pawnee braves again. Their behavior quite often took on forms that appeared illogical even to me.

Blossoms were sprouting along the Platte. Dainty prairie sunflowers and daisies and wild prairie roses were scattered in profusion among the grasses edging the trail. The day after the second marriage offer, walking along beside my favorite ox, Buck, I snapped out of my usual one-foot-in-front-of-the-other daze when I spied a sudden trail of petals. Inspecting the wildflowers along the path, I began to observe a certain pattern of wanton beheadings.

"Amelia?"

Amelia emerged from her own self-imposed trance to glance my way. For the first time in weeks I noticed her chin. Singular. There was definitely only one, molded smoothly and quite elegantly to her neck. Wildflowers weren't the only things beginning to blossom around here.

"Yes, Phoebe?"

I blinked and she was my big sister again, not some exotic beauty. "What do you think about, walking all these miles each day?"

"Think about? Books I've read . . . Lowell . . . things I'd like to write someday."

"Ever think about flowers?"

She took in those surrounding us. "They're pretty, but no. Not especially."

I gestured toward some decapitated specimens. "There are too many missing, and Timothy and Mary Rose generally collect them by their stems in whole lots. There's a mystery here, Amelia, and I intend to get to the bottom of it. Prod Buck for a few minutes."

Scampering forward, I followed the trail of petals till I came to the very root of the situation, as it were: Hannah and Sarah Kennan, desultorily leading their own oxen. I slowed my pace behind, unnoticed.

"Your turn, Sarah."

Sarah plucked a fresh, spritely daisy by her side. "He loves me, he loves me not. He loves me, he loves me not. . . ." Petals scattered until the heart of the ravaged blossom was discarded. "Oh, pooh, Hannah. He loves me not."

"My turn." A lovely wild rose bit the dust. "He'll return for me. . . . He won't." This flower had fewer petals. "He'll return! So, there, Sarah Kennan!"

I slipped quietly toward the rear of the line, shaking my head. Margaret O'Malley caught me three wagons before my own. She swiped at the dust on her face, uncovering fresh freckles.

"What's going on up there, Phoebe? And did you notice all those massacred flowers? Who in the world—"

"The twins." That was all I needed to say.

Margaret made a face. "I hope to heaven I don't turn so daft when a young man finally catches my fancy."

"We've still got time, Margaret. For which I thank Providence regularly."

Fortuitously, we didn't have to deal with the Kennans on a personal level except during noonings and our evening stops. How their mother kept her patience with them in between was a wonder. But Tabitha Kennan was a patient woman—or maybe just another ground down one. She hadn't quite got the knack of taking things in hand for herself since Captain Kennan's lamented departure back at the buffalo killing grounds.

Truth to tell, most of the women hadn't. They were having trouble understanding how droving the oxen all day, then still having to make the meals and deal with laundry and suchlike was quite the liberating experience Miss Simpson made it out to be. Ever so slowly, however, accommodations were being made.

The younger widows—Mabel Hatch and Helen Kincaid and Henrietta Vernon—had taken to sharing meals together. Mrs. Davis and Mrs. Russell looked to be considering similar arrangements. Miss

Prendergast mostly did for Miss Simpson, herself, and Zachary Judd. Miss Simpson most certainly did not expect to do any cooking. I suppose she thought her leadership role put her above such mundane necessaries. As for Mama, well, she mainly displayed her newfound strength of character by continuing to stoically deal with Papa.

It wasn't until we arrived at Windlass Hill above Ash Hollow that the main difference between males and females finally made itself obvious.

Windlass Hill was the first really steep grade on the Oregon Trail. By general consensus it cropped up roughly five hundred miles from Independence.

It didn't look like much at first, just another steady incline on the prairie. Buck and Bright and the other oxen were huffing a little on the way up. Of a sudden, they stopped. They had to. Two other wagons were halted ahead of us, blocking the track. They belonged to Mabel Hatch and Henrietta Vernon, and those two ladies were staring down at something, wringing their hands.

Amelia and I bustled up to reconnoiter the situation, only to stop dead ourselves.

"You see what I see, Amelia?"

Amelia pulled at her thick, dark hair distractedly. "I see a hundred-and-fifty-foot drop, Phoebe. How are we going to manage that? Worse yet—" She kicked at a clod of stone-hard earth between clumps of stiff, dry grass. "Worse yet, how are we to manage the true mountains beyond? Everyone's been talking about just getting to Fort Laramie, Phoebe. Nobody's said one single word about the mountains beyond!"

"Maybe they're scared to, Amelia. Maybe it's enough to finish one piece of the trail at a time."

Amelia stared at the seemingly hopeless piece before us. "Lord, but maybe men are good for something. At least they're strong!"

Miss Simpson finally made it to the edge of the precipice. She squinted down the incline, into the ravine below. "Just where the guidebook said it would be, all right. About a twenty-five-degree slope at the easiest angle." Her eyes darted back to two scraggly dwarf cedars near the rim. "Phoebe!"

I jumped. "Yes, ma'am?"

"Collect every length of rope from every blessed whitetop. Bring the lot here. We'll lower the wagons down one by one."

I inspected those two pitiful cedars in which she was obviously putting her faith. "You think they're going to hold up to the weight, Miss Simpson?"

"They're going to have to, Phoebe Brown. Unless you have a better suggestion?"

"No, ma'am." I scurried off with some alacrity. A moment of concern for Papa and the other two invalids slowed me. If they remained in the wagons, they'd likely be floating down that precipice on their heads. But was there any other choice? One problem at a time. I began gathering rope.

We let the Hatch wagon down first. Miss Simpson ordered two lengths of rope tied to its rear axle. The far ends of the ropes were wound around those little cedars. Next, Miss Simpson lined every able body in camp alongside those ropes in teams, just like playing at tug-of-war. For a wonder, Happy Hawkins convinced her husband to pull, too, but from the grin on his face I was fairly certain Mr. Hawkins mistook it for the baby game.

Everything organized to her satisfaction, Miss Simpson prodded the oxen to the brink.

"Ready, teams?" she yelled. *"Gee!"*

We could hear her thwacking at the animals, forcing them over the edge. Didn't need to hear it, though, the way that rope made a violent pull against the palms of my hands, cutting right into the skin. But we couldn't let that heavy Hatch wagon plow into the oxen. The rope had to slip through our hands inch by inch. Amelia was in front of me, holding on to the rope for dear life. Mama was behind me, already panting and praying for the strength of Samson. Off to my left, Miss Prendergast tugged so hard she dislodged the spectacles from her nose.

I never before had any inkling of how many inches there were in a hundred and fifty feet of rope. After those first two wagons were lowered safely down into Ash Hollow, I figured I'd not soon forget. The brush burns on the palms of my hands wouldn't let me.

It was our wagon's turn next. Flushed from the victory of helping to successfully ease two white-tops to safety, Mama solicitously propped extra pillows behind Papa's head. She made sure the remaining supplies and her cherrywood chest were strapped down good and tight. Still, Papa was aware of the ordeal to come. He developed a sudden fear of tight spaces.

"Ruth," he pleaded from the interior. "Ruth. If I don't make it down, see to it the girls are looked after in Oregon. Amelia don't look too shabby these days. Surely there'll be some man willing to vouch for her—"

"Stop talking nonsense, Henry. Nothing is going to happen to you."

"Ruth." Papa did not mean to let up, even embarrassing the family like he was in front of the entire train. "Ruth, not a heathen husband, either. I won't have halfbreeds for grandchildren!"

"I truly do not believe Amelia's interests lie in that direction, Henry. But even if they did, the results would still be God's children."

"Mama!" Amelia had gone beet red.

"Ruth, perhaps you've been spending too much time with the Scriptures—"

Miss Simpson finally put a stop to Papa's babbling. "Enough caterwauling, Henry Brown. You're impeding progress. Phoebe!"

"Yes, ma'am?" I presented myself with relief.

"Phoebe, you are going down with your father. It will be your job to protect his head and legs from unnecessary jolts. Elsewise the last few weeks of healing could go for naught."

"Yes, ma'am. Which part should I concentrate on?"

"The anatomy is up to you, Phoebe Brown. Just get on with it."

"Yes, ma'am." I began crawling into the wagon.

"And as soon as you hit bottom, loosen the

ropes and get yourself up here again. We'll need your hands for the other wagons."

"Yes, Miss Simpson."

Relief mixed with foreboding swam in me as I went for Papa's legs. His head and tongue I'd have to leave to the care of Providence. Mama connected the ropes to our wagon's rear axle and Miss Simpson tightened them. Through the open arc of the canvas in the front of the wagon I watched Amelia prod the oxen. There was a vicious jolt. I fell forward over Papa's splinted knees.

"Hell and Damnation, Phoebe! You're here to help, not cripple me for life!"

"Sorry, Papa." I righted myself. Taking a firm grasp of each of his outstretched feet, I held on tight. "But I am doing my best. Your cussing is hardly seemly."

"Yet appropriate," he lashed out. "Curses become the only escape from the frustration of my miserable existence." He yelped at another lurch. "More politic words are inadequate. Has your fine Miss Simpson consulted me on any of these maneuvers? Has she consulted O'Malley or Judd?"

"Apparently not, Papa."

Unfortunately, my attention strayed over my

father's head to the view through the front of the wagon. Lurch by lurch, we were teetering down Windlass Hill. Vertically. The oxen, practically on their noses, were scrabbling for footholds. This was almost as bad as the fording of the Kansas River. *Lord*, I prayed silently. *Lord, let this pass. I'll be more daughterly to Papa. I'll fetch and carry for him without complaint. I'll have the patience of Job—*

"Phoebe?"

I opened my eyes. "Yes, Papa?"

"My head is sliding out of the wagon. Stop mumbling to yourself and perform your duty, daughter!"

My hands tightened around his feet and pulled his body toward me.

"Tarnation! Not thus! You're pulling my legs out of their sockets! You've probably undone all my recuperating!"

"Sorry, Papa." Weren't we down yet? There'd been hundreds of minuscule jerks on the wagon, thousands of inches of rope played out. I glanced out to see Bright stumble around a jagged boulder. The wheels were not going to miss it.

"Brace yourself!" I yelled.

The jolt came, along with the ominous crack of breaking straps.

I froze. "The cherry dresser!"

It was suddenly loose, closing in on us, ready to tip over and crush us, snuff us out in the five hundredth mile of the Trail. With only a hundred and fifty more miles till Laramie.

Papa opened his eyes to see it coming, too. "I knew that dresser was a mistake. From the start. I told your mother—" A drawer swung out to smack him on the side of the head, and he was silenced.

"Papa—" But the jolts had stopped. We'd leveled off. "We made the bottom!"

I sprang out to untie the ropes and watched as they were snaked back up the side of the hill. Next I prodded the oxen into pulling the wagon out of harm's way. Buck and Bright had picked up a few bloody scrapes, but seemed otherwise intact. I crawled back in the wagon and jostled the cherry dresser back into its proper place.

"Papa?" I touched his forehead. "Are you all right?"

Sharp blue eyes flashed open below bristling brows. "That dresser goes. First opportunity."

"But you promised Mama—"

"It goes." He closed his eyes again.

Shaking my head, I scrambled back up the incline.

Miss Simpson practically swaggered around the campfires that night. She'd thought like a man and accomplished a man's job. So had the rest of us, but we hadn't either her brawn or her stamina. We were just bone weary. And Amelia and I had first shift on lookout, too.

We waited till the camp had settled down into wagons and tents and blanket rolls, then grabbed Papa's rifle and began walking around the perimeter of the wagons. The stock was all staked down, drowsing at their hobbles. A few spare ash trees drooped nearby in the evening heat. I swatted at mosquitoes.

"Well, I guess I finally learned why God made these ornery creatures." I spoke aloud, mainly to keep from falling asleep on my feet. Amelia consulted Papa's pocket watch for the tenth time.

"Only fifteen minutes used up. Another two and three quarter hours to go. . . . Why, Phoebe?"

"To keep us awake on sentry duty, naturally."

"That doesn't account for the other hours of the night, does it? When they whine and draw blood and drive a body nearly out of her mind."

"Still and all—" I slapped at another half dozen and was rewarded with a sharp pain in my bruised palm. "Mrs. Hawkins's ointments haven't started working on these rope burns yet, either."

"It takes a little time, Phoebe. Try not to be so impatient."

"Why?"

"Why what?"

We'd finished circling the wagons once and were starting on the next round. "Why should I be more patient? I prayed for patience this afternoon, but it didn't seem to help. Papa still swore at me all the way down Windlass Hill."

"Papa is in a difficult position—"

"And it's of his own making. It was his idea to leave everything and head for the Promised Land. Not ours."

"Never forget Lowell, Phoebe."

"I've never seen Lowell! Was it really as bad as all that, Amelia?"

Amelia shivered. "I would have been enslaved there for years, Phoebe. Bloating up like a balloon from sheer misery. And you would, too." She squinted at me through the dark. "Well, maybe you wouldn't have bloated up. You've a different nature and would have picked some other way to vent your discontent."

She held up the face of the watch to catch the moon's light. "Three more minutes gone. . . . Believe me, sister. It was nothing like a life. At least out here we can breathe. I only pray there will be no infernal machines in Oregon."

"What will there be in Oregon? Besides land? What will we do?"

"I imagine we'll do much the same as we did in Massachusetts. Only with a difference."

"What difference?"

"I fully intend to do my duty by Mama and Papa. Help set up the homestead. But after that—"

"What happens after that?"

"After that I fully intend to make some time for myself. This trip has been an enlightening experience. It *is* possible to break from Papa's stranglehold. At least in little ways." She stopped. "I mean to write."

"Those tracts under your mattress. The ones signed *Amelia*. Then they really were yours? All those phrases about showing 'the driveling cotton lords, the mushroom aristocracy of New England, that our rights cannot be trampled upon with impunity—' "

"Yes!" Her voice was a joyful affirmative. "To see one's words in print . . . Phoebe, you cannot imagine the thrill!"

"More thrilling than getting a husband? That's what you wanted at the start of the trip."

"Nonsense to that. At the start of the trip I wanted escape. A husband seemed a suitable solution. The last two months have taught me differently. . . . I do believe in the New Land I shall be my own woman. Leave the men for Hannah and Sarah to moon over like addled cows. *I* shall have my own voice!"

Admiration for my big sister flowed over me. To have found a path like that seemed a wondrous thing. There was no way I could have come up with a phrase like "driveling cotton lords." Maybe, hidden behind her calm facade, Amelia had already found her voice. I didn't bother to quibble over how she intended to get it into print in the wilderness. Instead, I gave her an impulsive hug in the darkness.

"I like you much more since you came back from Lowell, Amelia. I even begin to understand what you mean. Words might not be the right thing for me, but there'll be something out there! If we come to the New Land different from what we were—sort of reborn—surely that could change things. And not just for you and me, either. Maybe for Mama, too, and the other women. Only consider how strong we were when we all worked together today on Windlass Hill!"

Amelia opened her mouth as if to answer. I

stilled my steady pacing, waiting for the affirmation of my high-blown thoughts. Waiting for a sisterly outburst of affection equal to my own.

Her gesture turned into a yawn as she consulted the pocket watch yet again. "Only another two and a half hours on sentry duty, Phoebe."

SIX

A day later we got our first sight of Courthouse Rock. It was yet forty miles off, and not even directly on our trail, but already the sandstone butte jutted massively from the flat prairie. It looked just like some etchings of proud medieval fortresses I'd seen in a history book back home at school. That gave me something to think about most of the weary miles. Instead of a motley assortment of wagons, our party became an invading army, manned by ferocious Amazons ready to lay siege to the Black Knight waiting in his castle up there. Even a villain like that wouldn't have had a chance against our chief Amazon, Miss Simpson.

Considering the arid plateau lands around us—and the only potential enemies we'd met thus far—I suppose that fortress ought to have been some ancient Indian stronghold. Still, I had trouble imagining the Indians as true enemies. More reasonably, they should be wary of *us*, trouncing through their lands the way we were, using up their water and forage as if it belonged to us. Back in Massachusetts a body didn't graze his cows on a neighbor's fields without permission or rent. Sometimes it seemed to me those Pawnee could reasonably be asking for more than just Hannah and Sarah Kennan.

The next day, peering through the midday haze, I thought I caught sight of the needle-thin spire of Chimney Rock just beyond Courthouse Rock. I grinned with satisfaction at knowing the name for yet another landmark. Miss Simpson would have informed the entire train in good time, of course. But that was *her* time. She'd begun to parcel out information only when she felt it was deserving, like a little treat for good schoolchildren.

Unwilling to wait for her scraps, I sought knowledge in another place. I took to visiting with Miss Prendergast and Zachary Judd of an evening—in that brief period before bedtime, after the ritual footsoaking with the girls in the Platte.

Miss Prendergast had been a schoolteacher, too. She admitted as much. But she was another kind. It was like night and day, the difference between her gentle tutoring and Miss Simpson's more strident methods. Miss Prendergast was also the keeper of the duplicate guidebook. This guidebook would be presented and opened almost furtively each evening, for the pleasure and edification of the three of us. And each evening we would scratch off another fourteen or fifteen or even sixteen miles from the total still remaining to Fort Laramie.

We sat just inside the blacksmith's wagon, using up precious candles so that Zachary Judd might partake of the experience. He was always propped up on pillows, all big bones and slow drawl. Not that he was backward in any way. His eyes were alert and his smile sweet under a vast moustache as he beamed at Miss Prendergast. That smile lit up his entire homely face, clear up to his mop of curly black hair.

"And what will I be seeing with you tomorrow, Alice?"

Just like that he called her Alice, and Miss Prendergast blushed, each and every time.

But he really would be taking in the view, because Miss Prendergast had recently finished fixing up a kind of window next to his head. She'd cut through the thick canvas and would roll up a yard-wide section each morning. It was clever, and I suppose Amelia and Mama and I could have done the same for Papa, as the bulk of the cherry-wood dresser only took over one wall of the whitetop. The O'Malley girls could have done it for their father, too. Yet the result of such an unalterable action gave us pause. It wasn't because of the extra dust getting into the wagons, either. Deep down we were much more frightened of the increase in orders coming *out* of those wagons.

Miss Prendergast didn't have that problem.

"By late afternoon we should be crossing Pumpkin Creek, Mr. Judd. Maybe Emily will decide to camp there. And all day you'll have the delight of seeing Chimney Rock grow larger."

Mr. Judd. Why couldn't she call him by his given name, too? Was it improper, or was she too shy? My head swung between the two. What was there to be shy about? Mr. Judd was like a huge, friendly bear. He was about twice as big as the schoolteacher, his fists now crumpling his coverlet more like paws that ought to have a hammer or bellows clutched between them—or maybe a vast tree trunk. He grinned when he saw me staring.

"These hands be useless now, Phoebe girl, but come Oregon and a mended hip . . . well, they'll build a mighty fine house." He paused. "A house fit for a loving family."

Miss Prendergast blushed clear down to her neck this time. I decided to help her out of her fix. "How far yet to Fort Laramie, Miss Prendergast?"

Her eyes lowered gratefully to the guidebook. "Only seventy-five miles from Chimney Rock, Phoebe. With Scotts Bluff and Robidoux Pass between. Maybe a week."

"We'll be needing another early start, then, I reckon, to make time tomorrow." I was already crawling from the wagon, judging the two of them could use a little private time before Miss Simpson came to fetch Miss Prendergast, as she seemed to do each evening. "'Night all."

We did settle by Pumpkin Creek the following evening, but I didn't have time for either a leisurely soaking of feet or a visit with Miss Prendergast and her blacksmith. Amelia and I were set for the second watch and had to catch some beauty sleep beforetimes.

Lizzie and Margaret O'Malley had pulled the first watch, and they were shaking Amelia and me out of our blanket rolls beside the wagon entirely too soon.

"Leggo, Margaret," I growled.

"Get up and do your duty, Phoebe Brown!"

"Why? Nothing ever happens, anyhow. Waste of time, the whole enterprise." I burrowed deeper into my covers.

"Do stop fussing, Phoebe." Amelia was already

on her knees, apologizing to the O'Malleys. "Rising gracefully from sleep has never been Phoebe's strongest trait."

Amelia gave my hair a yank. She hadn't done that in years. I suddenly remembered why we'd never been the best of friends before her sojourn in Lowell.

"Lay off, Amelia," I snarled. "You're not my favorite sister anymore."

"Shall I pull it again?"

I rose, fully clothed in anticipation of the sentry chore. "Let's get it over with."

The night was heavy and chill at the same time. A mass of clouds coming from the north blanketed half the stars, sending tendrils curling around the quarter moon. Shivering involuntarily, I clutched more tightly at my woolen shawl.

"Strange how the prairie can be so hot all day, and turn cold in the middle of the night," I remarked in an attempt at resuming cordial relations.

"Hush, Phoebe. We don't want to wake anyone." Amelia adjusted the family rifle more comfortably in the crook of her arm.

Miffed, I straddled a wagon trace and stomped off into the wild beyond. Outside the boundaries of the circled wagons, the deep night seemed even more alien, the rising wind harsher. The next three hours were going to be a trial for certain.

How many more middle watches would I be responsible for until the end of the journey? As my brain was still a little sluggish, I worked out the calculations slowly. Almost fifteen hundred more miles, at fifteen miles a day. Better make that ten, figuring for river fordings, anticipated mountains beyond Laramie, and occasional layovers. . . . That would be one hundred and fifty more nights. A hundred and fifty? That had to be too many. It would get us to Oregon in November, after the snows had started. . . . Still, it was an easy number to work with. Stick with it and divide by three watches, then divide again by how many women?

A slight movement to my left destroyed all the hard thinking. "Amelia," I whispered. "Amelia. Is that you?" I tightened the shawl again. Amelia had the rifle and even if it was a worthless weapon, without it I felt naked.

A minuscule crunch from ahead froze me in my tracks. Was it the hobbled animals? Was it something—or someone—else?

"Amelia!"

Still no answer. She must have chosen to guard the other side of the wagons. What were sentries supposed to do if we did come across something unusual? Shout "Halt and present yourself"? With all her directives, Miss Simpson had neglected to address that possibility. What if it were something—a bear or a mountain lion—that didn't answer questions? Silly. I shook my head. Those creatures didn't live on the prairie.

Another crackle of dry grass caught my attention. Then again, what if it were a *someone*? A someone who didn't understand English? Out here in t' e middle of the night potential Indians became more mysterious and terrifying. Mighty fast.

I spun around at new noise. . . . Was it scuffling? Ridiculous. My imagination was merely overwrought. Caution, however, never hurt.

"Halt and present yourself!"

It was meant to sound ferocious, but came out as a weak warble. Little matter. In another moment, a different sound met my ears. A sort of hissing. Before I could piece the soft sounds together as the moccasin treads they were, a hand was over my mouth. "Amel—"

No good. The hand was firm and hard, smelling of animal grease. No way those fingers were Amelia's delicate, slender ones. I bit into them, hard. A soft grunt was my answer, then low words.

"Han-nah. Sa-rah. Where?"

I didn't need to twist my neck to know I was under the power of Wind Pony. Panther Claw, too. He had to be the second dark shadow busily and surely hobbling my arms before me, and my legs beneath me. In an instant I was helpless.

The words came again, and the voice brooked no nonsense. "Where?"

"If you'd only let me talk—" The thought came out loud, surprising me. Wind Pony had eased the pressure on my mouth.

"Speak!"

No point in getting mauled or worse over those twins. The girls wanted nothing more than their braves anyhow. I jerked my head toward the wagons. "The whitetop with the letters . . . that is, pictures on the side." The Kennan wagon was the only one decorated. *Manifest Destiny* was taking on stranger meanings all the time.

Some kind of a gag was shoved in my mouth, and I was let loose—loose to sprawl flat on my face. I had a sudden sympathy for the animals we tethered each night. It wasn't any joke being tied up so you couldn't move.

I lay there for a while feeling sorry for myself. Then I began wondering about Amelia. The

Pawnee must have picked her off first. Why hadn't *she* pointed them to the Kennans' wagon?

Miss Simpson crossed my mind, too. The Great and Wise Mother of Wagons of Women was not going to be pleased at her sentries' performance. Somehow the wrath of Miss Simpson seemed worse than kidnapping Pawnee. The head-mistress at my school in Massachusetts had had a similar effect upon me.

I pulled myself together. Leastways, I hunched up on my elbows and began dragging myself in the direction of the wagons. How Wind Pony and Panther Claw intended to spirit off those twins without waking the entire camp would at least be interesting to watch.

I bumbled into Amelia almost at the edge of the wagon circle. She was sprawled over Papa's useless rifle, breathing deeply, but not otherwise moving. Maybe they'd bashed her first and thought to ask questions later. Unable to do anything about that situation, I inched like a caterpillar closer to the wagons. My skirt and petticoats inched with me, hiking up to my waist. Forward on chin and elbows, hump my back, haul the fettered legs. I never felt so at one with Mother Earth before. At one with each blade of cutting, prickly grass, with each tiny pebble now grown monumental against my defenseless skin. It was not a method of locomotion I would recommend.

Someone had neglected to put out their cooking fire. It was a waste of rare and precious fuel, but the dying flicker cast some light on the Kennans' wagon across the circle. I rested from my labors next to a spoked wheel and focused on the two dark shadows entering the wagon. A body was hauled out, gagged and tied. It was inspected under the sky. I could almost see the look of disgust that passed between the braves. They'd snaffled a Kennan, all right, but it was the twins' mother. She was shoved unceremoniously onto the grass by the traces. The twins must be sleeping out tonight.

Stepping delicately over Tabitha Kennan's impotently jerking feet, Panther began to examine several bundled objects to the rear of the wagon. His head bobbed in jubilation as he nodded at Wind Pony. In a moment, dark hands were clamped over white faces and shanks of blond hair—silver in the night—were being freed from constricting blankets. Hannah and Sarah awoke with equal looks of surprise. How they would have responded next was never allowed to me to know. Working feverishly, the two braves soon had the girls trussed up worse than me, slung over their shoulders, and removed from the circle of wagons. All without making a sound.

I stared out beyond the wagons into the darkness as a peal of thunder split the night. It was Mrs. Kennan's twitching that finally forced me into action, though. It was kind of pitiful. Here was one moment the woman could have been forgiven a good swoon, and she couldn't do it. That made me think of how my own mother would feel if Wind and Panther had taken off with Amelia and me instead. Poor thing. She'd be stuck with nothing but Papa. And Mrs. Kennan hadn't even a husband left to fall back on.

I would have sighed if I could have managed it. Better yet, I would have yelled. Neither being a possibility, I swallowed hard and did the only thing left to me. I began banging the bottom of the nearest wagon with my head.

Thump . . . thump . . . thump.

My, but that did smart.

Thump.

"Who's there?"

Praise the Lord. It was Happy Hawkins.

Thump.

"Move over, Theodore. Something's going on out there."

I gave one more thump, just to keep her interest up. Any more and I'd be as useless as Amelia.

Mrs. Hawkins was emerging at last. I could tell by the wagon's groans and her hefty legs swinging within view. Pulling her nightgown decently down, she lunged from the wagon bed—directly onto the back of my outstretched legs. My scream was soundless, but hers wasn't.

"Merciful heavens!"

Mrs. Hawkins must have been putting two and two together. That was all I noticed before I swooned as bad as any Kennan. The last thing I remember thinking was that it was unfair to faint like that. I wasn't any silly Kennan female. Worse yet, I'd surely miss out on the rest of the action.

It wasn't dark anymore when I woke up. Then again, maybe it was. I was surrounded by blazing lanterns. Amelia was laid out next to me, still peacefully sleeping, and Mama was crying over both of us.

She obviously needed some comfort. "Don't fret, Mama. I'm right as rain, and Amelia will be, too—" I suddenly noticed I'd been cut loose from the Pawnee bonds and tried moving my limbs. Bad idea. Mama must have noticed the expression on my face, because she set in to another round of sobs.

"Do stop, Mama. I need to know what's happening."

A handkerchief delicately sped over her face and then she was hugging me.

"My poor baby. If we'd only made it sooner to Fort Laramie, this never would have happened. Just a few more days—"

"Mother. Please." I forced myself to sit up. Everything ached, from my head on down to my toes. The Pawnee had been one thing, but Happy Hawkins was entirely another. Had the woman any idea of the weight she was carrying around? I glanced beyond the lanterns to the rest of the circle. Everyone was awake and scurrying like madmen. We must have been next to our family wagon, because I could hear Papa complaining from within.

"What's happening, Ruth? Nobody tells me anything. Are the girls all right?" Thrashing sounds filtered out. "Blast! That cherrywood dresser got me again!"

Mama ignored him. "Miss Simpson is about to give chase with Tabitha Kennan and a posse of women, Phoebe. In pursuit of the twins. I only pray they may not be too late."

"Too late for what, Mama?"

She shuddered and dabbed at her eyes. "Just too late."

After what all I'd been through, a person would think Mama had other things to worry about besides my maidenly ears. Apparently she hadn't. I tried rising to my feet.

Mama grabbed for a leg. "What do you think you're doing, Phoebe?"

"Getting to our horse. I have to follow the posse, help them."

"Never. You've done enough this night."

My knees crumpled under me. Perhaps Mama had a point.

SEVEN

*A*melia had a lump on her head the size of a hen's egg in the midmorning light—and a headache to match it. I wasn't exactly feeling like a victorious Amazon myself. Methodically, I took stock.

The back of my own head was tender from meeting up with the floorboards of the Hawkins wagon. My chin was still bloody from trying to use it as a foot. Working along down my anatomy, both elbows were raw. I'd have to hunt for my missing shawl later, but in the meantime the sleeves of my red-checked gingham dress were in shreds. My ankles still held the impressions of Pawnee rawhide.

But Happy Hawkins appeared to have left her mark most forcefully. Although I did try, I couldn't see the backs of my legs. Amelia, however—between groans—assured me that Happy's footprints were turning the most putrid shades of yellow and dark purple. Right there on the upper part of my appendages that ladies were never supposed to refer to as thighs.

Marked for life. The wonder was that all the separate parts of the body still seemed to work. Under protest. I contemplated all of these outrages over a steaming cup of coffee Mama was kind enough to place in my hands. Mama herself looked like she'd had better nights. Her eyes were still red and swollen, there were fresh worry creases across her brow, and her shoulders hunched forward as if she hadn't the will left to pull them back.

"It could be worse, Mama," I tried.

She poked a newly gray hair behind one ear. "I'm sure I don't see how, Phoebe. No amount of resourcefulness could prepare me for this. My only offspring, the daughters I have labored so hard to raise as proper young ladies . . . set upon and mauled by savage Indians! All because your father wanted to see the elephant."

"I don't appreciate having my name taken in vain, Ruth. Particularly when I cannot defend myself."

Papa never missed anything from inside that wagon, no matter how he protested to the contrary.

"You have not seen the state of your children, Henry!"

"What about my state? I'm mauled every blessed day by this cherrywood horror of yours—"

Mama's voice rose in intensity. "That dresser will be relinquished only over my dead body, Henry."

There was some indecipherable mumbling from inside the wagon, but luckily the sore subject of the cherrywood dresser was dropped once more as the sounds of hoofbeats reached our ears.

"The posse!" I perked up. "They're coming back!"

"Either that, or the entire Pawnee tribe in warpaint is arriving to finish us off," Amelia moaned. "Which at this point might be a blessing in disguise."

I forced myself to my feet and hobbled to the edge of our whitetop. It was situated to the south and the gap in the wagon circle opened onto the vast plateau of the prairie. The riders were coming in fast from around the great bluff of Courthouse Rock.

"Sorry to disappoint you, Amelia, but there's not a single feather or bare chest in sight. It's the posse. Miss Simpson is in the lead . . . and they must have gotten the twins back, because the two spare horses have wriggling bodies tossed over their saddles."

Amelia had had enough of the Kennan twins. She remained supine on the grass, nursing her head. "Are you quite certain they're wriggling, Phoebe?"

"Absolutely. And even from this distance I'd judge it was with fury."

Miss Simpson oversaw the unloading of the twins with ill-concealed choler. She'd apparently had enough of the two as well.

"Shove Hannah this way, Happy."

A blond bundle was dumped onto the ground. A second lump soon followed. The remaining females dismounted from frothing horses to gather around the twins. Even Tabitha Kennan, their own mother, turned to Miss Simpson for instructions on what to do next.

There was a pregnant pause as Miss Simpson considered.

"I suppose we might as well untie them," she finally spat out. "Can't very well keep them bound up for the next fifteen hundred miles."

Nevertheless, she stayed Mrs. Hawkins's hand. I guess she was in dire need of venting her spleen, for after taking a deep breath, she laid into those twins.

"Hannah and Sarah Kennan," she fumed.

"You've been responsible for jeopardizing every member of this wagon train." Beady eyes drilled into the two girls in question. "Your behavior has been silly, frivolous, and flighty. You led on those young men, knowing the inappropriateness of the situation. I truly cannot say I blame those Pawnee braves for what happened. I blame you for making eyes at them, waving at them—"

How had Miss Simpson caught on to all of that? Then again, headmistresses were known to have eyes in the back of their heads. And Miss Simpson's were sharper than most. I watched the twins, waiting for some sort of apology. Of course, they were still fully gagged—this time with bandannas—but there was nothing like remorse in their eyes. Hannah and Sarah were still spitting mad.

"—and the two of you only fifteen years of age!" Relentlessly, Miss Simpson proceeded with her lecture. "I feel sorry for your poor mother, but I'll have to remand you to her care. I cannot merely expel you from the wagon train, as I would from a school of better behaved young ladies. . . ." Miss Simpson paused for her clincher. "Merely remember that all eyes will be upon you in the future. I'm in charge, and I'm getting you to Oregon. If you wish to marry there, that's your funeral."

She turned to Happy. "Unloose them. The rest of you get ready to move. We're behind schedule for Fort Laramie."

It was sheer misery getting through the rest of that day. And most of the misery wasn't from bodily aches, either. It was from not knowing the details of how Hannah and Sarah had been caught.

I fairly burned after the information. Amelia did too, although she protested to the contrary.

"Honestly, Phoebe." Amelia tossed her head, too late remembering its delicate condition. "Why should I care to know the sordid details of their sordid elopement?"

I turned from the wagon seat to make sure that Papa was, indeed, still napping. He was snoring like a babe. Good. Time to verify some fine points. "Is it a true elopement if the marriage ceremony gets interrupted? Surely there wasn't time for a proper ceremony before Miss Simpson rescued Hannah and Sarah—"

Amelia was clutching her hen's egg again. "Who knows. Who cares."

"And what kind of ceremony would uncivilized Indians have? Would there be a ring? Or maybe just an exchange of beads or something? And do you think Hannah and Sarah would have gotten their ears pierced like Wind and Panther? I did admire those earrings of theirs. . . ."

I ground to a halt at the expression on my sister's face. Part annoyance, mostly pain. Sitting up on the wagon seat "recuperating" didn't seem to be working. Mama had insisted, but peering through the dust haze ahead, I could tell Mama wasn't faring much better with her oxen-prodding task. Maybe several hours of jostling atop the wagon was enough.

"We might as well take our chances on our own feet for a while, Amelia. Mama doesn't seem to be doing too well, either."

I creaked upright and swung off the seat, jarring every muscle as I hit the hard ground. Dramatically seizing her head, Amelia followed suit.

Lizzie and Margaret O'Malley had been members of the posse. I tried to catch their attention between wagons, but apparently their da was keeping a tight rein on them after their recent adventures. And we never even stopped for the nooning, having started too late in the day to begin with. So it was plod and plod some more until Miss Simpson finally burned out her wrath and called an evening halt.

Amelia and I finished struggling with the oxen's yokes, then stumbled back to the wagon. Mama had already hauled out the fry pan and even had a few flames started in a pile of buffalo chips. She took in the two of us briefly.

"I'll do the supper tonight. Get over to the river, both of you."

"Thank you, Mama!"

"Maybe I'll get some details from Mrs. Hawkins," Mama added. "But should the O'Malleys have further comments . . ."

I was already limping off. Amelia, a freshly wet rag strategically positioned on her lump, was following.

Margaret was already waiting for us.

"What took you so long, Phoebe?"

I raised my skirt. "Want to see Mrs. Hawkins's footprints?"

Margaret oohed a little, but not nearly as long or as satisfactorily as I would have liked. Apparently her news was more exciting.

"All right, then, Margaret." I flounced my petticoat and skirt back down. So much for glory. I hadn't even gotten to point out my chin and elbows. Or my sore head, which had really saved those twins from a fate worse than death. "What happened? Spit it out. Every word of it."

Margaret waited for Lizzie and Amelia to remove their boots and plunk their legs in the river. Clearly the twins would not be joining us this evening. Suspense suitably built, she launched into the story.

"The Pawnee's horses must have been waiting just beyond camp, Phoebe. Four of them. We couldn't miss the spot. One of those flashes of lightning lit up the sky. And there—big as life—"

"—were the leathern strips Hannah and Sarah had been bound with. Discarded," Lizzie continued, blue eyes asparkle. "Only imagine, Amelia, the twins rode off with those Pawnee *willingly*!"

"Galloping through the night, their golden hair astream. Off to unknown adventure . . ." Amelia forgot her head for a moment.

"Amelia Brown, you never approve of what they did!"

Amelia dunked her rag in the muddy river and held it against her bump again. "No, Lizzie . . . but it would make a lovely story."

"Just wait," Margaret interrupted. "Sure and we've hardly begun."

"Well," I pressed. "What happened next?"

"By the stars and the occasional flashes of lightning, Miss Simpson tracked them. As dawn was breaking, we rode over a rise, and there, below us, the Pawnee village was spread out, big as life."

Lizzie wrinkled her nose. "Stronger than life, too. Mangy dogs, naked, unwashed babies . . . the whole place was awake and reeking."

"Hovels!" Margaret added. "Jesus, Mary, and Joseph, the dirt was thicker than coming over from Ireland in steerage."

"Watch your tongue, Margaret O'Malley! And how could you be remembering that? You being hardly four during the voyage—"

"I remember, Lizzie. I do! The fearful seasickness for sure. At least the Pawnee village was on solid land. But those tiny mud houses—"

"Whoa!" I broke in. Someone had to clarify things. "How long did you get to look on Wind and Panther's village? And how in bright heaven did Miss Simpson pry the twins loose?"

A sudden yowl of outrage came from upcurrent. Timothy and Mary Rose O'Malley were tumbling in the Platte, pulling each other's hair.

"Mercy. Worse than wild Indians, they are. Will those two never stop?" Lizzie was already on her feet. Margaret followed, and by the time the youngest O'Malleys were separated and subdued, Mama was ringing the supper bell.

I turned to Amelia in frustration. "The telling is taking longer than the rescuing."

Hannah and Sarah were still nowhere to be seen, but at least Mama had garnered a few further facts. She shared them as she dished out our meals.

"The twins were being measured up for wedding dresses when Miss Simpson and our party arrived at the village. Beaded buckskins, Mrs. Hawkins said. The two fought like wildcats, not wanting to return. . . ." Mama stopped to hand me my tin bowl.

As far as I was concerned, that supper could have waited forever. "And?"

Mama was already back at the fire, scooping out a share for Amelia. "It seems Miss Simpson convinced the Pawnee chief that she was sister to the Great White Father in Washington. And if *she* was not pleased by the marriage, *he* certainly wouldn't be, either. Furthermore, *she* would see to it that *his* displeasure would be expressed by sending an entire troop of soldiers to attack the village." Mama actually grinned. "Mrs. Hawkins said Miss Simpson was quite impressive."

"Miss Simpson would be. What happened next, Mama?"

"The posse bundled up the girls—had to actually strap them to their mounts, like you saw—and returned to camp."

"That's all?" Amelia was distinctly disappointed. The denouement was not nearly romantic enough for her.

I was disappointed, too. What had happened to poor Wind Pony and Panther Claw? I dug into my stewed buffalo jerky and grimaced at the soreness still in my jaws. "Still and all, it would have been a wonder to see that Pawnee village. Son of a gun! Worth an eyetooth, at least, for the chance."

For some reason, that innocent comment seemed to upset Mama. She quivered visibly as the evening coolness set in.

"Phoebe, dear, I'm afraid this journey is bringing out the less civilized aspects of your character. Please try to comport your thoughts with more refinement."

"How in the world does a body comport its thoughts with refinement, Mama?" I put down my spoon to brush dust from my cheek. "Especially in a wilderness with wild Indians and all?"

Mama sighed. "If I were sure, I'd be addressing

the situation. Things were so much simpler in Massachusetts."

"But Massachusetts didn't have Indians. And now I'll probably never get another opportunity to study them. You *were* upset by my having to leave the Young Ladies' Seminary back home, Mama. It appears to me that Indians could be just as interesting to learn about as European history, or mythology, or—"

Mama tightened her shawl, but it didn't seem to help her shiver. "Thank God we are almost to Fort Laramie and beyond the territory of the Pawnee. I earnestly pray we may never set eyes on such barbarians again!"

Mama's prayers went unanswered. The very next afternoon, as we wended our way past the spiral of Chimney Rock, a thin trickle of dust appeared on the horizon to the north side of the Platte River. By the time we maneuvered our wagons into a circle that evening the dust had become a moving camp of Indians.

I ran to Miss Prendergast for a favor. "'Evening, ma'am." I stuck my head through Zachary Judd's window. "'Evening, Mr. Judd."

His wagon had been settled with a fine view of

the river, and the blacksmith was straining his neck to take in the sight across the way. Unfortunately, he was already using what I'd come to borrow.

"'Evening, Phoebe." He pulled the spyglass from his eye. "I'm not sure what tribe they be, but they're different from the Pawnee."

Miss Prendergast was rapidly paging through Thomas J. Farnham's *Journal of Travels in the Great Western Prairies*, her spectacles slipping from her nose as she squinted at the words. She had an entire chest filled with such books. "The Pawnee are a settled tribe," she finally announced. "These people are obviously nomadic. Did you get a good look at their travois, Mr. Judd?"

"Those poles trailing behind their horses, loaded with supplies? Hundreds of them, Alice. Some even pulled by dogs. A bunch of the women seem to be carrying their papooses and goods on their backs, too."

"Poor dears!" Miss Prendergast exclaimed. "They must be widows, or wives of unsuccessful braves. I'll warrant their men are riding in comfort, though."

Zachary Judd gave the spyglass another peep. "You be right as always, Alice."

Miss Prendergast's finger stopped over a long paragraph in small, heavy type. "Sioux. They must be Sioux. Oh, dear, there are several varieties. It says here they rendezvous for big powwows this time of year, usually around Fort Laramie."

My head followed the conversation between the two of them, while my legs jiggled with ill-concealed impatience. There was that fine spyglass in Mr. Judd's hand, and he was hardly using it. He finally noticed.

"Would you like to borrow the glass, Phoebe?" He glanced toward Miss Prendergast. "It would be all right, wouldn't it, Alice?"

She smiled. "Phoebe is quite responsible."

The spyglass was already cradled in my hands. "Just five minutes, I promise. Down by the river, so I can get a closer look."

"Not too close, Phoebe," she warned.

"No, Miss Prendergast. Thank you, Miss Prendergast."

Hannah and Sarah had finally slipped from their mother's grasp. They were sprawled stomach down in the grasses at the shallow river's edge. So were Amelia and the O'Malley girls. I slid down beside them, spyglass in hand. Before I even got it near my eye, though, Hannah had snatched it.

"Just for a moment, Phoebe. Please?"

"Have a caution, Hannah. It's not mine—"

But Hannah was already in another world.

"*Ooh*. Sister. There's a brave who's almost as fine as Wind Pony! Well, maybe not quite so fine—"

Sarah grabbed at the glass and plastered it to her own eye. "There are hundreds of them! Getting off their ponies. I do believe they intend to set up camp right across from us! That tall one coming down to water his horse has more claws around his neck than Panther!"

I stared over the twins' heads at Amelia and the O'Malleys. They were as dumbstruck as I. Here were the Kennan twins fresh from their abduction, rescue, and public embarrassment by Miss Simpson. Here they were, without even a how-de-do or a thank-you to Amelia and me for the beatings taken in their interest. And what were they doing? Readying themselves for more Indian troubles.

"Sarah Kennan," I yelled as I pulled the spy-glass from her face. "Sarah Kennan, for shame! Have you no feelings? No decency?"

Sarah was genuinely startled. "Whatever are you referring to, Phoebe Brown?"

Amelia, on her other side, answered for me. "She's referring to those two young braves you led on, and left with broken hearts. Barely twenty-four hours ago you fought to stay with them! How could you even look upon another young man?"

"Glory be, and another savage, at that," declared Lizzie.

"Oh, pooh." Hannah tossed her golden hair. "Sarah and I decided today that there's more than one young man in the world."

"That's right," agreed Sarah. "And *thousands* of Indians!"

"Maybe not all as nice as Wind Pony and Panther Claw, though." Disgusted, I moved a full yard away from the nearest twin and finally got the spyglass to my eye.

"Son of a gun!" I let out a long, low whistle, never even knowing before that I could. "Wow. These Sioux are all painted up. And the men are going at those tin saddlebags draped over their horses. What do you suppose is inside?" One of the braves swigged as I watched, then let out a jump and a whoop. "Not water," I decided.

Through my glass, the faces in the dying light took on strange and ominous overtones. I shivered the way Mama had the evening before. Slowly I moved the spyglass from my eye. "They're coming toward the river. A bunch of them. They could wade across easily. I'm getting out of here."

←«»→

"Firewater!" Miss Simpson spat out with disgust. "White man's whiskey." She was now in possession of the spyglass and was inspecting the campfires spreading in the dark across the river from us. "I'm afraid it's going to be a long night.

EIGHT

*M*iss Simpson was right again, even if I did
hate to admit it. I tossed and turned in
my blankets for hours as the sounds of drums and
chanting and stomping feet floated across the
Platte. That firewater had surely riled up our Sioux
neighbors. The Indians were having one terrific
celebration.

At some point I must have drifted off, but
nightmarish, flame-haloed faces kept haunting my
dreams. I even fancied a steady beat of drums and
hair-raising yowls. When those phantasms grew
larger than life, for once Amelia didn't need to
jostle me awake. I rose of my own accord, bleary-
eyed and exhausted, just as dawn was breaking.

Dangling my boots by their laces, I stepped
over sleeping bodies and wandered past the circle
of wagons to the edge of the river. I was planning
on settling down in my nightgown right there to
inspect the silent tipis across the water when I
noticed a movement to my left. Parting the grasses
with some hesitancy, I breathed a sigh of relief to

find little Timothy O'Malley standing nearby. He must have been half asleep, too, for he was wading in the river in only his britches, staring fixedly across its width.

I spotted what had caught Timothy's attention. Knee-deep across the Platte stood another little boy. A Sioux boy, naked but for a loincloth.

As if in silent agreement, the two of them began pushing through the waters toward each other. I knew Timothy could not swim, and I knew that although it was mostly shallow, the Platte still hid a few vicious currents and surprisingly deep spots. Yet for some reason I held back. It was only as the small Indian yelped and slipped that I moved into action.

"Timothy!" Tossing down my boots, I swept into the water to haul Master O'Malley from danger.

"Lemme go!"

"I will not!" I plunked him safely on the bank. "And if you move an inch, I swear I'll tell your da!"

That started up a sniffle, but I ignored it and turned toward the river again. Where was the Indian boy? My answer came ten yards downstream. A small arm was flung through the surface, but no head. The poor youngster had caught a current, and it didn't look as if he could swim any better than Timothy.

Without thinking, I plowed back into the river. A sneaky current caught me, too, and I found myself toppled full into the cool waters. Luckily my nightgown was the summer one and only cotton, but it still tangled my arms and legs ferociously. I couldn't pull it off midstream, so I stopped struggling with it and launched as best I could into an overhand stroke I'd taught myself in the cow pond back home. Praying the little Sioux hadn't already drowned, I finally caught up with him.

He was an unexpectedly small bundle, and limp in my arms. Finding a foothold at last, I struggled to my feet and ended up on the north side of the Platte. The Indian side. There wasn't time to dwell on that. I was too busy upending the little fellow and shaking him by his sun-browned legs.

"Come on, doggone it, spit up that river!" I shook some more, then lay him down to pound on his back. The sudden gush, when it came, told me he'd swallowed more Platte than was entirely healthy. I pounded some more until he was heaving, and gasping, and beginning to cry—just like any normal little boy might after such an adventure.

"Thank you, Lord!" I breathed.

I finally raised my head to a shock. Half that Sioux camp must've been wakened by my antics.

They stood around me now, the effects of the previous evening's carousing making their faces blank. Or maybe that was just a Sioux's natural expression. Except for one woman pushing through the crowd. As the group parted, she cried out and leaped for the youngster. His mother, obviously. I smiled.

"More or less safe and sound, ma'am. But he oughtn't be allowed to wander by the river without supervision."

More blank stares. I touched the little fellow once more and edged away from the crowd to the river. The crossing seemed longer this time, with all those eyes on my back. But I made it, grabbed Timothy's hand, and marched him back to camp.

Well, I did get a few thank-yous for my swim. Mainly from the O'Malleys. Since young Timothy and I were both sopping wet, the rising camp could hardly not notice that something had transpired. So then I had to explain to Mrs. O'Malley and the girls.

Mrs. O'Malley commenced to alternately wring her hands and smother Timothy with hugs. Obviously she thought the apple of her eye was the one almost drowned, not the Indian boy. Come to think of it, without my nightmare, that could have been the case. Meanwhile, Mr. O'Malley was yelling from inside the wagon for someone to take his belt to the boy and teach him a lesson he'd not soon forget.

Margaret was forced to fetch the much-feared implement of torture, but Mrs. O'Malley merely whacked it against a wagon wheel a few times out of sight of her husband. Timothy, being no dummy, howled in perfect time. It seemed to me the O'Malleys had gotten this little ritual down to perfection in the brief course of their lord and master's recuperation. Maybe Papa wasn't half bad at that. At least he'd never required this form of punishment to be perpetrated upon his off-spring.

Miss Simpson was not long in catching wind of an event in her camp. She was soon striding over, still tightening the no-nonsense knot of her hair, frowning at my own dripping mop and nightgown.

"What mischief have you gotten into now, Phoebe Brown?"

"I guess I wanted a closer look at those Sioux, Miss Simpson." My quick answer was imprudent. Luckily, Mrs. O'Malley saved me.

"You'll not be yelling at this angel from God Himself, Emily Simpson. She just saved my only son and an innocent wee Indian lad from drowning to death."

Miss Simpson received more details than she wanted and turned away. "I hope you haven't upset that tribe, young lady. It is highly desirable to keep them on their own side of the river." She sniffed. "Do get yourself into more decent attire."

Our wagons were creeping closer all day to Scotts Bluff, another mountain-sized sentinel, but this one with a subtle difference about it that I couldn't pin down. The buffalo grass was taking on a stunted look, too, and spiky plants Miss Prendergast called yucca had begun to crop up. There was also a sprinkling of wild currants and chokecherries across the prairie. Miss Prendergast had her herbal guide out during the nooning and pointed them out to me.

"They may not be as sweet as cultivated berries back home, Phoebe, but they are perfectly edible."

I sampled one and puckered up. "They've got a tang, all right. Still and all, they'd make a difference from buffalo jerky in the supper pot."

Miss Prendergast tasted for herself. "Perhaps *with* the jerky, Phoebe. I was reading about how the Indians mix such berries with dried meat and animal fat to make a traveling food they call pemmican."

I'd heard of more tantalizing dishes, but made a mental note of it nevertheless. "With the sugar and flour gone, I guess we can't really expect to be making pies out of the berries." I nodded toward the spikes of yucca scattered about. "Nothing they're good for, I suppose?"

Miss Prendergast sighed. "If we lacked rope, hemp could be made from those broad, fibrous leaves. . . . Nothing good to eat, though, my dear."

"Figured as much. There's already too many of them about. Guess I'd better fetch something to hold sour berries in."

Amelia and Mama and I took it by turns to lead the oxen and pick berries all that afternoon. By stopping time, directly beneath the hovering shadows of Scotts Bluff, we had a fair collection. Mama was testing a currant, deciding what to do with it for supper, when a commotion broke out in the camp. I raised my eyes from the berries to spy a delegation of Sioux braves making for the center of camp as if they owned the place.

They were ferocious in aspect, and all decked out, too, but differently from the Pawnee—no scalp locks for one thing, but full heads of long black hair braided down their backs as nice as you please. Considering the advanced ages of most of the men, I decided it couldn't be marriage on their minds.

They stopped smack in the middle of the circle and waited, arms folded. The Sioux tribe had been matching our own pace most of the day, but I'd been too busy with improving our diet to pay much attention. Now I stared with the best of our party. But not for long. Miss Simpson had already bustled over to the group. Happy Hawkins, unprepared for once, stood midway between her wagon and the men, obviously trying to decide if it would be politic to fetch her rifle. Probably since our visitors hadn't any weapons, she gave up and joined Miss Simpson.

Hands were raised in the obligatory "hows," and the palavering began. That went on for a while, Miss Simpson's face taking on a curious expression. Finally she backed away a foot or two and motioned in the direction of our wagon.

I glanced at Amelia and Mama. "Do you suppose she wants us?"

"Phoebe Brown!" Miss Simpson snapped.

"Then again, maybe it's me she wants."

I walked decorously toward the group, wondering why. Had it something to do with the little

Indian boy? He hadn't gone and died on me, had he? My footsteps slowed. If he'd gone and died, I'd be responsible in the eyes of his poor mother, not to mention the rest of his tribe.

"Hurry up, Phoebe!"

Please, Lord. He was a cute little thing. Not nearly ready yet for the happy hunting grounds.

"Phoebe!"

I loped the final distance, heart atwitter. "Yes, Miss Simpson?"

Shockingly, Miss Simpson cracked a smile and put her hand on my shoulder, pushing me forward. "This is our young heroine. Phoebe saved the boy."

"Fee-bee." An ancient Indian peered at me. His face was very wrinkled. Our eyes locked and he broke away first to nod to a younger man to his side. About Papa's age this one must be.

"Fee-bee," the second intoned. "You save my son, Yellow Feather."

I gulped. "Yes, sir. I hope he's doing all right."

Happy Hawkins broke in. "He's doing just fine, Phoebe. These gentlemen came to thank you. Seems Yellow Feather is the chief's son, and a chief-to-be. They want to invite you to supper. A feast in your honor."

The weight of the world that'd been lodged on

my shoulders a mere moment before vanished directly. I grinned. "My pleasure! How about my big sister and my mother? May they come, too?"

There were ponies waiting on our side of the Platte to waft us across in style. The final party was a little bigger than anticipated, though.

Besides myself and the Sioux there was Mama, distinctly frightened, and Amelia, intrigued. Then there were a few O'Malleys. It seemed Yellow Feather had ordered that Timothy be invited. Mrs. O'Malley outright refused to go, turning white clear through her freckles at the prospect. Lizzie and Margaret were thus delegated to the task of seeing that Timothy was neither abducted nor otherwise subverted by the heathen. The Kennan twins had been fluttering around the edges of the excitement the whole time, their mother with a solid grip on each. They begged to be included, too, but Miss Simpson firmly squelched that.

On the north shore of the river, strong arms helped us dismount. In moments we were surrounded by a throng of Indians as curious about us as we were about them.

In the excitement of the moment, Lizzie and Margaret had entirely forgotten their former intentions to disguise their hair, and they became great successes with their red mops and freckles. It seemed as if that entire tribe wanted to touch hair and match skin colors with them. Miss Simpson may have considered the whole inspection business improper, but the Sioux were ever so polite about it.

At last the old wizened fellow—apparently respected and feared both—broke up the doings to lead me to a campfire. Everyone followed, and we were seated in a circle around the flames. Directly in front of us was the largest tipi, its hides beautifully painted with birds and hunting scenes. Yellow Feather's father diverted my attention from the designs when he launched into some English, attempting to explain the proceedings.

"I am Black Tail of Hawk." He nodded toward the ancient one. "Medicine man is Arrow Shield. Arrow Shield pray now and we smoke sacred pipe. Sacred tobacco, *chan sha'sha*, mixed with sweet herbs."

Mama, to one side of me, clutched my arm. I smiled. Sharing the sacred pipe sounded exciting to me. I only hoped I wouldn't choke on the smoke and embarrass everyone. . . . But now Arrow Shield was catching my attention.

He slowly rose within his robes and turned toward the sunset. It was an especially impressive one. Long streaks of purple worked around the orange ball of fire clear across the sky, till they were cut by the brooding hulk of Scotts Bluff.

Arrow Shield offered up in his two hands a fantastically carved pipe—some kind of pinkish stone it was, with a stem almost two feet long. Pointing the stem first toward the rapidly lowering sun, then toward Scotts Bluff, he began to chant. Singing that way, he was no longer old, but strong and powerful and impressive.

The sound of Arrow Shield's voice was spellbinding, even if the only distinct word I caught was *wakan*, repeated a number of times. Maybe that was their name for the Great Spirit. . . . And those words, they thrust through the evening sky with authority. Surely God could hear them through the sudden hush. It truly was like being in church, only nicer under the open heavens.

With a last nod to the sky and to the bluff, the old man lowered himself, shrinking back into his robes. Someone fetched a coal from the fire and he lit the tobacco. He took one puff and handed the pipe to Black Tail of Hawk on his left. Another puff and the pipe moved on. Slowly the pipe made its way around the circle.

Finally it was in my hands. I felt its weight, fingered the intricate designs, brought the stem to my mouth. One puff only, that seemed to be the rule. A pity. I would have liked to hold the beautiful thing longer.

Amelia, who had choked out her puff moments before, gave me a nudge. "They're waiting, Phoebe."

"Don't rush me. A sacred pipe is special."

I inhaled. Aromatic vapors overcame me— hints of cherrywood, like Mama's dresser, and a subtle taste of wild huckleberries. I let go of the smoke and relinquished the pipe to Mama. She merely touched it to her lips with ill-disguised distaste and passed it on. My head reeling slightly, I grinned across the fire straight into Arrow Shield's eyes. I'd swear the old man winked back at me.

The pipe finished and the sun gone down, Black Tail of Hawk spoke again.

"Fee-bee. Come."

Mama clutched at my skirt hem as if I were going to my doom instead of just around the fire. "Come on, Mama," I whispered. "I'm the heroine, remember?"

I walked past my own family. I walked past the O'Malleys. Timothy was already nodding off. I continued past Yellow Feather's mother and a few other Sioux to where Black Tail of Hawk was waiting. Yellow Feather stood next to his father, straight and serious.

"Fee-bee," his father said. "Yellow Feather had sister, but no more. He desires new sister. You."

I smiled down on the solemn boy. "I'd be honored. I always hankered after a little brother myself."

Black Tail of Hawk nodded. "It is good. We make you blood sister."

I wanted to ask how he intended doing that, but several drums outside the circle started up a steady *tom-tom* beat. I held my tongue. It might not be appropriate to speak in the middle of a ritual.

Black Tail of Hawk reached for my right hand. His other hand held Yellow Feather's small fingers. Arrow Shield rose majestically, flashing a knife. It was an ancient knife, chipped from stone. I caught Mama's gasp across the fire, but ignored it as the blade slashed over my palm. Curious how sharp an ancient Indian knife could be.

Unflinching, I stared with fascination at the droplets of blood oozing from the wound. With equal interest I watched Yellow Feather's hand being cut. In a moment his father was holding our two palms together, and the medicine man was chanting over us. Black Tail of Hawk broke into a smile. It lit up his craggy face.

"It is done. Now you are Swift Fish, sister to Yellow Feather. Sister to Dakota Sioux." His raised arms encompassed the two of us. "Swift Fish is under our protection forevermore. May the spirits watch over her."

Swift Fish. I played the name over in my mind. It made a certain kind of sense. It was a nice compliment. I stood taller as Arrow Shield took my hand and smeared the wound with a greasy ointment. It took the sting right out of it. Invited to sit down next to my new little brother, I gave him a hug, and the main business of the evening commenced. Women started bringing on the food.

I guess that feast was better than eating buffalo jerky stew back in our own camp. It was certainly more memorable.

The first course was a tremendous bowlful of something which looked like gruel, but was thicker and stickier. I watched carefully as Yellow Feather dipped his fingers into his own bowl, rolled a huge lump of the stuff between thumb and forefinger, and popped it into his mouth. I followed suit. *Umph.* It was a mess of some kind of cloying boiled corn. Stuck right to the roof of your mouth. Yellow Feather was enjoying his, though, so I dug in for more. Before you knew it, that little boy had cleaned up about two quarts of the stuff and was casting longing glances at my hardly touched bowl. I snuck a look around at my Indian companions. No one seemed to be paying much attention, so I swapped bowls. Yellow Feather beamed and plowed in.

The next course was a generous amount of some kind of potatolike root. These had been roasted and weren't too bad. I managed three or four, being careful to save a goodly portion for my new brother. That made him even happier. It seemed a shame this relationship wasn't going to last longer than the night. Yellow Feather was much better behaved than Timothy O'Malley ever was. I could have gotten used to him.

The drums increased in tempo as a third course arrived. This was obviously the *pièce de résistance*, as I'd heard Miss Prendergast say once or twice. It was meat. Fresh meat. Where had the Sioux found fresh game? Between their dust on one side of the river and our dust on the other, even rabbits had been scarce the last few days on the trail.

I raised a nice-sized haunch to my mouth. Before biting into it, I peered across the fire. Were Mama and Amelia receiving the same celebrity treatment? Nope. Looked as if they were still working through about three quarts of mush each.

Sniffing the aroma of the meat in anticipation, I allowed my mouth to water a little. I wanted to savor the moment. I looked beyond the light of the fire. There were watching Sioux, and something else, too. Dogs. Dozens of them sitting in expectant rows, probably waiting for scraps. Indians certainly were fond of their dogs.

My teeth met the crisp flesh of the roast meat and closed down. One dog—a lot like a coyote it was—started in with a mournful howl. Its neighbor joined in. I chewed thoughtfully. The meat was a little stringy, but the flavor wasn't bad. Gamier than rabbit.

I glanced at Yellow Feather. He was devouring his serving with relish. All the dogs were carrying on now. My stomach suddenly lurched. With absolute certainty I realized what I was eating. One of the family dogs.

Black Tail of Hawk chose this moment to take notice of me.

"Swift Fish. You do not like our food?"

Luckily it was too dark for him to see my face clearly. I picked up the haunch again. Did I call him Papa now that we were related? Perhaps not.

"It is past delicious, Father of Yellow Feather. Thank you for the honor." I had to eat that entire haunch under his searching eyes.

At some point Yellow Feather had disappeared from my side. Probably when he realized he wasn't getting any of my dog. Now I saw him waking Timothy O'Malley from where he'd fallen asleep in

Lizzie's lap. That signified my honorary feast was finished. There'd be no dessert.

Dancing began between the other campfires. Drums beat, rattles shook, whistles soared, and the Sioux braves cavorted with enthusiasm and grace. I remained straddled on my legs, Indian fashion, watching Yellow Feather and Timothy whoop around the edges of the entertainment with the other Sioux children, watching a million stars fill the sky and almost settle atop the looming blackness of Scotts Bluff. I knew it was time to go home when my eyes were so filled with the wonders of the strange night that I could no longer force them open.

Loggy with sleep, I nearly slid from the bare back of the Indian pony I'd been hoisted upon. It was Yellow Feather's mother who caught me. I never was properly introduced to her, but she smiled on me and handed me a parcel. Then our horses were wading south across the Platte.

NINE

Blinking at a sun that was halfway up the sky, I struggled awake the next day. It was late. Amelia was fussing by the breakfast fire, much too languidly for our usual pace.

"'Morning." I yawned widely. "What's going on? We should've been on the trail hours ago."

"Miss Simpson called a day's layover."

"Here? With us only four or five days from Fort Laramie—and everyone so anxious to get there?"

"She said the stock needed resting, and the grass was not bad."

I digested that for a moment. "Truth to tell, I've seen better grass. What she really meant, I'll wager, is that she'd prefer a little more distance between us and those Sioux."

Amelia made no answer, so I trotted beyond the wagons to stare across the Platte. Sure enough, they were gone. The plain was empty. It looked desolate that morning next to the stark vastness of Scotts Bluff. I suddenly missed the Sioux. Especially my new little brother. Would I ever see him again? Then a fresh thought occurred to me. I brightened and raced back to our wagon.

"That parcel, Amelia. The one Yellow Feather's mother gave me last night. Where is it? I was asleep on my feet, and it was too dark to see it properly anyway—"

Amelia pointed to the rear of the wagon and I scampered around to pop my head in. "'Morning, Papa." Sure enough, he had it in his hands. My present.

"Good morning, Phoebe. Or should I be calling you Swift Fish from now on?"

"That won't be necessary, Papa. It was only an honorary title. May I have my present?"

He tossed it at me from his pillows. "*Heathen* wares."

I jumped to catch it, hoping it hadn't been damaged. "You'd rather I'd let Yellow Feather drown?"

He growled. "Don't know what's come over my women. Ignoring me. Fraternizing with the enemy."

"The Indians aren't our enemies, Papa. Not unless we choose to make them so."

He must not have really wanted to talk about Indians, because he changed the subject on me. "Do your chores, Phoebe. Then collect fuel for the fire. Your mother was complaining that we're almost out of buffalo chips. A hot meal is, after all, one of the few things I have left to look forward to."

"Yes, Papa."

But I didn't go after buffalo chips directly. I didn't go back to the river, either. The women were all beginning to congregate there to wash their dirty linens. Instead, I left the circle to wander a distance into the prairie and settle down to inspect my treasure.

And it was, indeed, a treasure. It was a small bag sewn from softened skins, lovingly beaded in intricate, colorful designs. I opened the leathern clasp to peek inside. There lay another treasure.

"Oh, my."

I spoke aloud without knowing it. In my hand was a delicately crafted doll, dressed in buckskin, with a tiny papoose on her back. "Oh, *my*."

This doll had belonged to Yellow Feather's sister. I knew it without being able to explain how. Just as I'd known about the meat last night.

What would her name have been? Would she have been my age now? Like me, she'd probably be too old for playing with dolls. She would have saved this one nevertheless, secretly loving it, keeping it for her own daughter some day. Now it would be saved for my daughter. A tear trickled down my cheek and splattered on the leathern face.

"Hey, Swift Fish!"

My head shot up. Tarnation, it was Hannah Kennan, with Sarah right behind. Using my new name like it was some kind of an insult. Thousands of miles of prairie there were to get lost in, and they had to stumble across me. Quickly wiping my face, I stuffed the doll back into its home, then hid the purse behind my back.

"How about going for a swim?" Hannah asked.

"No, thank you. I had my bath yesterday." Both twins knew they weren't wanted, but crowded in on me anyway.

"Tell us about the Sioux last night, Phoebe."

"Were there any handsome braves?"

I wasn't yet ready to have the mystery of last night trampled upon, either. "Sorry, girls. It was too dark to see much. Besides, I've got to go after buffalo chips now. Shouldn't you be helping your own mother?"

It wasn't as if I really ever wanted to see any buffalo again in my entire life, but hauling that half-filled fuel sack a fair piece of the afternoon made me wonder where they'd gotten to. By rights there ought to be tons of chips drying under the hot sun from last year's herds.

I peeked in the sack again. Wasn't enough fuel

there to last more than a few meals. What were we to cook with after it was gone? I squinted around the prairie. There certainly weren't any trees to be had, either, except for one scraggly pine jutting from the very top of Scotts Bluff itself. That must have been there a couple thousand years, at least. For one rash moment I actually considered climbing up after it with Papa's ax. Right up that four-hundred-odd feet of cliff face. There did seem to be ledges, eroded by the prairie winds. . . . I took another look. Silly idea. The sun must be going to my head. I really ought to be wearing my bonnet more, but I hated bonnets.

Still, I studied the bluff more carefully. Through the shimmering layers of heat it had a look that gave me sudden shivers. Yet something about it beckoned, too. Arrow Shield the medicine man had pointed his pipe toward the bluff last night during his prayer. Did it mean something special to my little brother's people?

I'd probably never know. Shouldering my sack, I headed back for camp.

Mama and Amelia were still down by the river working on the laundry. I carefully emptied buffalo chips for safekeeping into what had once been our bean bin at the foot of the wagon. I was doing it quietly, so as not to wake Papa, who was napping the afternoon away. I hated to think of his renewed energy level once we got him to Oregon and healed. After all the sleep he was getting, the man would be unstoppable. I reached into the sack for another chip. It slipped out of my hands.

Papa's even snoring broke. "Whatzit . . . who's there?"

"Phoebe, Papa."

An eye opened. "Hope you got enough chips to justify waking me, daughter."

I upended the rest of the sack into the bin. Papa raised his head. "Can't see them chips crowding over the top, yet."

"That's because the bin's barely a quarter filled, Papa."

"You been lollygagging all day, girl? A baby could've collected more chips than that!"

"I can't find what isn't there, Papa. The big herds just didn't come through this way. Can't say that I blame them, either. There's something about that bluff—"

"Don't lay any of your nonsense on me, Phoebe. I've put up with entirely too much of it lately. You go back out there and do your duty. *Find* some fuel. That's an order!"

"But, Papa—"

"And don't come back until you do!"

A direct order was hard to outright disobey. But where to find the fuel? As I backed away from the wagon my eyes lit again on that one lonely pine atop Scotts Bluff. If that was the way Papa wanted it . . . I reached for the ax and set off.

The first hundred feet up weren't really that bad, aside from the handicap of hefting Papa's ax. I finally rested on a ledge, pulled off a petticoat, and rolled it into a belt to fasten the tool next to my waist. After that it was easier keeping my balance. It was also easier trying to figure out why I was climbing Scotts Bluff. Truth to tell, it had less to do with Papa's order than with the strange feelings I'd been having since smoking the sacred pipe and my blood sister ceremony with the Sioux last night. Then there'd been that gift this morning. I really needed to know more about my own personal Indians, and I had an idea this tremendous lump of earth rising from the dry prairie was tied in with them some way. But how?

Past the halfway point a strange thing happened. I began hearing things. I cocked an ear and looked up. Never down. That would be outright stupid from this height.

What was that sound? There was the constant

wind, of course, stronger at this height than on the prairie. But there was something else, too. A kind of soft, howling lament. Wolves? They were always off in the distance nights, but seemed to keep that distance. What would wolves be doing on Scotts Bluff in broad daylight? I shook it all from my head and kept climbing.

Something rustled above me. I raised my eyes to stare straight into those of a huge buzzard. It winked its hooded red pupils and gaped its curved beak evilly. I swatted at it.

"Shoo! I'm not carrion yet!"

Still, I cringed as it swooped away. With such a wingspan that buzzard could've carted me off. Nearly. I climbed some more, beginning to doubt the wisdom of taking on this pitiless rock.

I paused to swipe at the rivulets of perspiration nearly blinding me before struggling higher. Another ledge. I pulled myself up to rest. I couldn't see the camp from where I sat, just the endless ribbon of the Platte moving east, and the infinite prairie rolling north, past where the Sioux had camped last night. You couldn't tell they'd ever been there. They'd left nothing behind. I moved the hand shielding my eyes to grip at the ledge above, then stopped dead.

I'd been resting next to bones. *Human* bones.

Had to be. There was a dried-out skull grinning at me, a row of loosened teeth surrounding it like a necklace.

When that next howl came, I skeddadled.

At that point, I ought to have shimmied directly down, straight down to the good flat earth again. Instead, I went up. Up and up, with the furies pushing me. Never let it be said that a mere mountain, a dried-up skull, and an old buzzard could keep Phoebe Brown from accomplishing what she'd set out to accomplish. Forget Papa's orders, this was becoming a matter of principle.

Howls, chanting voices, and ghostly drumbeats tore at my eardrums. When I reached the top of Scotts Bluff, I scarcely noticed. Trembling, I nearly tripped over a small cairn of pebbles.

I picked up a pebble, then something under it. A bone, inscribed with symbols. There were more bones beneath the first. I studied them: circles were etched within circles, rays extending from them; small stick figures with tiny spears; even something that looked like a buffalo running from an arrow. Someone had been up here before me—a long time ago. Maybe Yellow Feather's ancestors. Maybe I'd been right about this bluff being special for the Sioux. Was it their voices surrounding me? Their spirits? Could the spirit of Yellow Feather's sister be here with me, too? If she were, could I do anything for her? It must be a terrible sadness not being allowed to grow up.

"Yellow Feather's sister?" I spoke aloud without thinking it out. "I'm sorry I don't know your true name. But mine is Swift Fish, and I just want you to know that your little brother is fine. I'd look after him some more if I could, but I'm just passing through. I have a feeling, though, that he's going to grow up strong and brave. I'll treasure your doll and papoose, too. And try to be worthy of you. . . ."

The voices quieted, as if digesting my words. I carefully reburied the offerings in the cairn and finally looked to that lone pine a few yards away. In the looking, I suddenly noticed how the wind had picked up as the voices stilled. Now it buffeted me with passion, trying to blow me right off the hand-kerchief-sized peak of Scotts Bluff.

Not so scraggly to me now, I crawled on all fours over the tiny summit to reach the pine. I hugged the wiry trunk. I kissed its scarred bark. It was alive.

"Well, now, tree." I was still hugging it, afraid to let go. I forced my head around the trunk, then pulled back with alacrity. The pine was directly on the edge of the precipice, its roots grasping at nothingness. Still, I clung to a bough.

"What do I do now? A few whacks with Papa's ax and you'd topple directly over the cliff. I could pick up your leftovers on the bottom."

The wind shifted again, carrying another faint howl.

"Then again, maybe you and the Sioux spirits have an agreement up here to look after each other. Papa's ax could drop over the side just as easily, couldn't it? Can't chop down a tree without an ax."

My fingers were busily unknotting my petticoat belt. The ax slipped out. I hefted it and swung it mightily toward the edge, then let go. The wind died.

"That's a relief for all of us. I guess you can get on with surviving another thousand years, tree. . . . And the spirits of your friends can rest easy, too. I won't say a word to a living soul about what's up here. They wouldn't understand, anyway. Me, I'll just try to get back down this mountain again."

I signaled a good-bye in the direction of the cairn. Then I chose another path to the bottom, one that wouldn't take me past the grinning skull. I didn't realize till I was nearly down that it was also a path within direct view of our camp. When I got tired and sort of tumbled and rolled off the last fifty feet of Scotts Bluff, I opened my squinched eyes to a surprise.

A slew of women were standing there, wringing their hands. Luckily one of them wasn't Miss Simpson.

"Phoebe!" Miss Prendergast found her voice first.

I got up to dust off my bottom and see what was left of my petticoat. "Yes, ma'am?"

"Phoebe! What were you doing atop Scotts Bluff?"

"Well, I was in charge of the family fuel, and that tree up there seemed like the only fuel left around."

Mrs. Davis, and Mrs. Russell, and the trio of young widows shook their heads and muttered.

"Scandalous!"

"The child nearly killed herself!"

Mrs. O'Malley kept on praying over her rosary beads. Happy Hawkins went after her husband who was eyeing the path of my downward tumble with interest. Must've looked like fun to him.

"Phoebe." Miss Prendergast pressed one hand against her heart as if she were having palpitations—but she wasn't anywhere near old enough for them, and much too pretty, even if she did wear spectacles.

"Are you all right, Miss Prendergast?"

She came to her senses, grabbing my hand. "Am *I* all right? . . . And all this time I've been believing you deserved that name."

"Which name? Phoebe or Swift Fish?"

"Your christened name, for 'bright one,' of course. I guess you earned the other all by yourself."

"Beg your pardon, ma'am, but what are you going on about?"

"I'm going on about your total lack of sense in climbing that, that *thing*. Didn't you realize there's a certain aura hanging over Scotts Bluff? Men have died here, Phoebe. Violently."

I shook the image of that skull from my mind. Surely she couldn't know about *him*. "Who, Miss Prendergast?"

"Hiram Scott, the mountain man whose bones were found directly at its base. The bluff was named after him. His party's canoes overturned in the river upstream, near Laramie, and all their powder was spoiled—"

"Goodness," I broke in, still fussing with my skirt. "We weren't the only ones. Kind of makes you feel less . . . less stupid, doesn't it."

"There are different degrees of stupidity, child. Their rifles useless, the group had to forage for roots. That's when Hiram Scott took ill and was abandoned. Returning the next summer, the same party found his bleached bones *here*, sixty long miles from where they'd left him—"

"He crawled all that distance alone?"

Miss Prendergast was breathing more evenly again. "He did, Phoebe. And who knows what other secrets this menacing mountain hides? Thank God you survived the climb!"

Well, I guessed I knew what some of those other secrets were, all right. And I also guessed that God had been keeping an eye on me, too. The Lord *and* the sacred spirits of my little brother's tribe. Black Tail of Hawk had put me under their protection. And Arrow Shield—well, I kind of suspected he would have been proud of my recent encounter, him being in the spirit business and all.

"I appreciate your concern, Miss Prendergast. Too bad I didn't know about Mr. Scott before the climb. Right now, though, I've got to go find Papa's ax. It slipped and fell over the edge before I could cut down that pine tree."

Miss Prendergast squinted at the tiny tree atop the bluff. "You risked life and limb for nothing, then."

I had other ideas about that. I ignored the stiffness overcoming my limbs from the recent ordeal to smile at the tree. "Perhaps."

Even with Mr. Scott's doleful bluff looming over us, the camp was in unaccustomed spirits that night. Maybe it was because all the women could look forward to clean petticoats and smallclothes the next morning. Maybe it was because we were so close to the fort that was going to solve a whole bunch of our immediate problems—like fresh stores and gunpowder. Maybe it was even a little relief at my having survived that climb. Mama and Amelia had missed the entire show, but were suitably informed by the neighbors before I could explain. By the time I'd returned to camp with the ax, Mama just hugged me as hard as I'd hugged that tree. Papa didn't say another solitary word about my fuel-gathering abilities, either.

Now I watched Happy Hawkins set her husband down by a central fire.

"Don't you move, Theodore. I'm going to fetch a treat for you."

He beamed hopefully like the small boy he'd become and sat there patting his knobby knees until she'd returned with a fiddle. I never did see a lady play a fiddle before. Apparently no one else had, either. After running through a rousing tune, practically the entire camp was gathered around Happy, gawking.

"Play us another, Happy!"

"Please do!"

In the brief silence that ensued while she was thinking up another, I heard my name called from a wagon. Ears perked up, I caught it again. It was Mr. Judd for sure. I headed right over.

"Yes, sir?"

"Ever play a jaw harp, Phoebe?"

"I've never played any instrument, Mr. Judd."

"Well, seeing as how I can't join in the festivities, it seemed to me a shame to let mine go to waste." He held up a tiny iron horseshoe-shaped object. "Made it myself. Here's how it works." Placing it between his lips, he pulled with his fingers at a thin wire attached to the bottom of the horseshoe and let out a twanging that set me to giggling.

"Are you sure I could do that, Mr. Judd?"

"You could do anything you set your mind to, Phoebe." He grinned. "Like taking on that mountain today. Although it was downright scary watching you through the spyglass." He handed me the harp. "Here now. Take it over by Happy and let me hear you really go at it."

"I'll do it for you, Mr. Judd."

He sank back into his pillows. "Thank you. It might take my mind off the itch in my leg."

"You get them, too, just like Papa?"

"I assure you, I get them too."

By the time I got back, Happy had launched into "Yankee Doodle." That's where I got my next surprise of the evening. Rising up above everyone else's voice was Margaret O'Malley's. Jaw agape at the sheer, unconscious, soaring loveliness of it, I forgot to test that harp till the very last refrain. It hardly mattered. There were a lot more songs still coming for me to practice on.

TEN

*M*aybe the layover had been a good idea after all. The following morning women and oxen alike took on the next piece of trail with renewed heart.

I was of several minds about seeing Scotts Bluff gradually dissolve into clouds of dust behind us. By this time it was all mixed up in my head—part mystical Sioux spirits, part learning how far I could push myself, part melancholy death. I certainly wouldn't care to be deserted by my comrades in this wilderness.

It was worse than wilderness. Yesterday's scrappy prairie was turning into badlands before our eyes. Gouged out, rock-hard, barren badlands. At the nooning Miss Simpson finally admitted the fact.

"Well," I overheard her saying to Mrs. Hawkins, "I had hoped to cut off a few miles by proceeding directly along the river, but there's hardly any grass to speak of—"

Happy Hawkins was half listening while she

stared at her front wheels. She finally raised her head. "That last hole near tore off my iron rims. They'd better have a working blacksmith at Laramie!"

Miss Simpson took Happy's battered rims as an acknowledgment. "You're agreed, then? We'll have to take our chance on water and detour south to pick up Robidoux Pass after all. There is Horse Creek coming up in about twenty miles, then we'll be back on the Platte to Laramie."

Happy turned to wipe a dribble of watery gruel from her waiting husband's chin. "You've got the guidebook, Emily. But I don't think my rig can take many more of these godforsaken gulches. Have you had enough dinner, Theodore? Good. You may go and play with the children now."

Mr. Hawkins had turned out to be useful to someone. During the long treks each day he hung about the youngest O'Malleys, picking flowers or pretty stones with them and keeping them out of harm's way from wagon wheels and oxen's feet. There was something percolating yet within his brain, for he always seemed to sense when Timothy or Mary Rose or Maureen were about to get into danger.

Miss Prendergast had taken to calling him one of God's Fools, and told me how long ago in

Europe such people were fed and cared for by villagers. She said they believed these fools were so innocent that they had a direct line to the Almighty. I looked on Mr. Hawkins more respectfully after that.

We clattered over a scarred ridge into Robidoux Pass about two hours past the nooning. Strange how land hereabouts could change like day to night in a few miles. We found ourselves in a circular valley filled with loose, sandy loam. The grass still wasn't anything like it had been a few weeks back, but there was grass. We soldiered on.

Without a river to plunk our feet into that evening, Amelia, Lizzie, Margaret, and I sat in a patch of rough buffalo grass outside the camp, having made good and certain first that it harbored no hiding snakes. Margaret was pretty good at snake chasing. She went about it with enthusiasm.

"Here, snake, snake, snake! Here, snakes!" She'd call this out, just as if she were gathering hens for their feeding back on the farm. Her voice, melodious when singing, was raucous enough at such times to scatter even the grasshoppers. Of course, while she was calling, she'd also be pounding like a dervish at that grass with a whip, carrot hair swirling, a mad look in her blue eyes. It set me into fits of giggles, this exorcism of hers. I almost wished an errant snake would slither out. It surely would be interesting to see what Margaret would do *next*.

Thus, not worrying about snakes, I was sprawled out enjoying the early evening coolness with the others. Sucking on a blade of grass, I made believe my bare toes were luxuriating in the cool Platte.

"'Evening, all!" Hannah's voice, filled with false gaiety, made us jump.

"We brought a peace offering." That was Sarah, too sugary by half.

As we'd been avoiding the twins for days, four sets of shoulders stiffened for the expected on-slaught.

"I'm sure there was no need—" Amelia began.

"Sister and I decided there was." Hannah flounced down in our midst, a small jar in her hand. "Here. It's our very last."

Lizzie reached for the jar curiously. "Very last what?"

"Why, the very last of our cucumber and lemon face cream, of course." Sarah explained as if it ought to be obvious. "Didn't you wonder just a teensy bit how Hannah and I have kept our lovely complexions?" Her heart-shaped face jutted forward, waiting for approval.

Amelia's response was as dry as her sunburned face. "Now that you mention it, no."

The twins were too thick by far to accept that rebuff. "Do try a dab on your face, Amelia. And you on your nose, Lizzie. It works wonders with freckles."

Maybe Lizzie's freckles were a sorer point of vanity than I'd anticipated. She lifted the lid from the jar and poked a finger in. "Well, if you'll be insisting that way . . ." She wafted the cream past her face for a sniff. Very tentatively, she dabbed some on the tip of her nose in one white lump.

"Dear me, Lizzie. Have you never owned a face cream? Like this!" Hannah removed the jar from her grasp and spread the cream around Lizzie's pert nose and across her wide cheekbones with practiced ease. She sat back to consider her labors. "Did you ever try a beer and egg shampoo on your head, Lizzie? Not now, of course, as there's neither to hand. Just something to consider for later, in Oregon. I do believe it would calm the frizz and bring out the deeper tones in your hair."

"Do you think so? My hair has been the trial of my life. And Da makes a passable barrel of beer, at least by his account. He's even brought hop seeds for the new land—"

"Our daddy used to enjoy his beer, too." Sarah was suddenly turning paler and reaching for her handkerchief. "Not that anyone else was allowed to taste it. So Hannah and I thought, well, we women ought to get some use of it."

A chortle slipped unaccountably from my throat. There seemed more ways than one to get around the males of the world. Perhaps the Kennan twins were harboring more resourcefulness than their feckless natures let on. I touched my peeling nose. "If you promise not to say a single word about Indian braves of any tribe whatsoever, I might let you test some of that stuff on me."

Sarah stashed away her handkerchief in anticipation as Amelia and Margaret began roaring with laughter. We painted each others' faces until the jar was empty and the sun set.

Our party reached Horse Creek for the next day's nooning. I watched the thirsty animals guzzle their fill. By evening we'd be on the Platte again, and in another two days—God providing and no more surprises—we'd be at Fort Laramie.

Fort Laramie. I toyed with the name in my head. It was a good name. Strong, yet a little exotic, like each new mile of this land. Could it succor us as we hoped?

Leaving the animals, I idly studied our surroundings. We certainly could use a little succor at this point—the whole lot of us in the party. Even with enough present nourishment, all the women were taking on gaunter aspects, as if their faces had been redesigned by a whittling knife. The oxen had a similar look, while the wagons shrieked and moaned louder each day. And contrary to what Happy Hawkins had said way back on the buffalo massacre grounds, our meat supply was barely going to get us to Laramie, never mind China.

Was that a dark cloud hovering on the western horizon? Thoughts of Laramie disappeared. I ran across the camp, screeching to a halt before Miss Simpson.

"Ma'am?"

She was tucking into a bowl of Miss Prendergast's pemmican with apparent enthusiasm. She took her time chewing a mouthful, swallowed, then gave me her attention. "Yes, Phoebe?"

"Have you looked to the west, Miss Simpson? There's something—"

She was already on her feet and fetching the spyglass. Pulling it all the way out, she fixed it to her eye, stared, then carefully telescoped it again. "Not a storm. A herd of something, maybe elk.

The shapes aren't squat enough for buffalo. As it won't do us an ounce of good without gunpowder, I judge it can be ignored."

"Oh. Sorry to disturb you, Miss Simpson."

I walked back to my own family fire, not looking forward to what I'd find in the pot. Whatever it was had to be less tempting than even Miss Prendergast's pemmican. Wouldn't fresh elk taste good about now! I began to understand Amelia's craving for lye soap not so long ago. Anything but more buffalo jerky stewed, boiled, or fried. I slumped down on my haunches.

"Why, whatever is the matter, Phoebe?"

"Nothing, Mama. I've only been wondering how we're going to shoot us any fresh game even after we've got working gunpowder. I'll bet not a single female aside from Happy Hawkins even knows how to load a rifle."

Mama planted her hands on her hips. "Daughter, if we've survived raging rivers and buffalo and heathens, I don't see why we can't do a simple thing like teach ourselves how to shoot."

"Ha!" Papa barked from the wagon. That sliver of waterproofed cloth separating him from us was getting thinner every blessed day. "It takes a strong shoulder and a strong eye. It takes a man!"

"You'd better begin praying that isn't so, Henry," Mama answered with admirable restraint. "Or else this train will never make it to Oregon. And in case you haven't figured it out, that means *you* won't make it, either, dear."

I grinned. I liked it when Mama was feeling sassy. "Let me have a big helping of that muck, Mama. It's probably better than what the Indians fed us the other night."

"Why, thank you, Phoebe. I do believe it has a little more flavor myself. I added some of our last pepper and salt and a few of the herbs we've picked along the way. With the proper victuals at hand I'm convinced I could outshine any Indian squaw. I did pride myself on keeping a fine table back home."

It was Amelia's turn to tidy up after the noon dinner, so I strolled down to Horse Creek, then along its banks for a small distance. I was perked up considerably by what met my eyes past a bend. *Somebody* knew I was still in need. I let out a whoop. A bunch of people came running, Miss Prendergast in the lead.

"What is it, Phoebe?"

Mrs. Davis gasped. "Look! Piled up there along the banks. Good as gold, it is!"

"The child's found driftwood!" Mrs. Russell clasped her hands.

"And just in time!"

Well, you'd think I truly had found gold by the way all those widows swooped down. Like a passel of buzzards they were. But this bunch bypassed the hovering stage of my acquaintance on Scotts Bluff and commenced directly to picking the carcass clean.

I stood watching the display with awe, wondering whether to elbow in on them to get a share for the Brown family. The rush lasted all of five minutes. Even Timothy and Mary Rose carted armfuls back to their wagon. Then the weathered wood was gone, every blessed splinter of it. I turned to Amelia, who'd just arrived and was hanging on to a few spindly sticks.

"Perhaps you might consider tempering your enthusiasm should you ever make another such discovery, Phoebe."

"You may have a point, Amelia."

Miss Prendergast lurched up from the streambed with her load, glasses askew. "Nonsense. Phoebe's first instinct was correct. We've got to help each other, else perish."

As my own arms were free, I solicitously readjusted her spectacles. "Yes, Miss Prendergast."

←—«»—→

Horse Creek was shallow and clear as we rolled our wagons across its seventy yards. I didn't even bother riding on the front seat with Mama and Amelia. I simply tucked up my skirt and petticoats, pulled off my boots and waded alongside the whitetop. The creek had a sandy bottom, and schools of tiny minnows darted around my ankles, wondering if I were something edible; too skittish to really try a nibble. Across the creek the plains stretched out again, covered with silvery-gray, low shrubs as far as the eye could see.

Now it was Miss Prendergast's turn to become excited. Even several wagons to the front of us I could hear her gentle voice raised well above its usual volume, expostulating with Miss Simpson.

"But Emily dear, this is priceless! It looks like sage and smells like sage. It *must* be sage. You've noted how quickly the terrain changes. I must harvest some of these herbs for future use before it all disappears!"

"We've at least six miles to make before evening, Alice. I cannot stop the train for mere *sage.*"

" 'How can a man die who has sage in his garden?' That's an ancient Arabian proverb, Emily. Only consider the good this might do our invalids. I'll grant you the plants have already begun to bloom and thus are a trifle beyond their prime, but *sage tea*, Emily. . . ."

I gave Amelia an apologetic look across our lead team. "May I go and help Miss Prendergast?"

"What?" She was already far off in some other world. "Very well, Phoebe. But not for the entire afternoon."

I skipped ahead. "I'll take on those oxen, Miss Prendergast. I'm sure you're a better judge of proper sage than I am."

Her smile was all the thanks I needed.

"I'll teach your mother how to make sage tea, Phoebe. And gather you an ample supply as well." She fetched a gathering basket and was off, humming to herself. "Won't this help ease Mr. Judd's aching hip!"

Miss Prendergast had been as convinced of her rightness as Miss Simpson generally was of her own. By camping time that evening, though, we'd left the vast fields far behind. The overall pungency of endless sage had passed from our nostrils, leaving only scattered plants, dry and past their prime. This didn't seem to stop the stock from grazing upon it.

Meanwhile, Miss Prendergast was busily tying her harvest into neat bundles to hang from the inside rims of her whitetop. She was also boiling up a caldron of sage tea. In all frankness, it reeked to high heaven.

"Here, Phoebe. You shall have the first taste of my brew." Miss Prendergast passed over a brimming ladle. I held it in front of my wrinkled nose, trying not to breathe in the fumes. People certainly went a long way for health. Hoping to delay the first taste, I blew at it. But as Miss Prendergast was eyeing me expectantly, I finally had to take a sip.

"Well?" she beamed.

I swirled that tea inside my mouth for a brief second. *Tarnation.* I spat it out forcefully, the ladle clattering to the hard ground. "No offense, Miss Prendergast, but I think I'll leave its therapeutic values to Mr. Judd and Papa and Mr. O'Malley."

"Oh, dear. By rights it ought to be sweetened—"

"Miss Prendergast, not even ambrosia would make this tea palatable. Excuse me." I raced for the nearest water bag, cleared out my mouth, and drank deeply to forget. When I turned back to the campfire, Miss Prendergast herself was tasting from the ladle. Her reaction was possibly more ladylike, but ended in the same result. Then she was attacking her chest of books, rooting out her herbal.

"Sage . . . sage. Here it is. Complete with a

sketch. Fetch me one of those plants, Phoebe."

"Yes, ma'am." I stood nearby while she ticked off similarities between the organism in hand and her illustration.

"Aromatic leaves, yes. Same smell—near that of mint—yes. Same coloring, yes." She looked up. "Yet this western sage has coarser roots, and I never have imagined it capable of growing wild in such profusion. The taste ought not to be bitter. Let me examine that leaf again." Miss Prendergast groaned. "Similar, yet subtly different." She snapped shut her herbal.

"What's the final result, Miss Prendergast?"

She sighed. "The final result is that nothing is as it appears in the West. I should have suspected that true sage would never prosper in such alkaline soil. Where, oh, where was my mind?"

"Probably fixing on trying to cure Mr. Judd faster, ma'am."

Miss Prendergast began a dilly of a blush, then hid her face from me as she walked over to her fire, struggled with the caldron, and got it far enough away from the flames to upend on the ground.

"There. Thank you, Phoebe. For aiding me this afternoon in my folly, and for stopping me from poisoning the entire train."

"Anytime, Miss Prendergast." I nodded toward

all her laboriously bundled fake herbs. "What'll we do with them?"

She was flopped on the ground, head in hand. "Consign them to the flames of ignominy."

That western sage did burn nicely, and sent a deceptively perfumed odor over the entire camp, much different from its smell when boiled. It lingered long after I'd tucked into my blankets, and I drifted to sleep with the incense in my nostrils.

ELEVEN

*W*e spent our nooning at Cold Springs the following day, but did not tarry long. We took time merely to force nourishment into ourselves and to freshen our water bags. Fort Laramie was less than twenty-five miles farther up the Platte River, and our hearts and bodies longed for it. Four hundred miles we had journeyed without the aid of our men—four hundred difficult and sometimes treacherous miles. Although there were fourteen hundred still to traverse, I'd wager none of us females were losing much thought over them. Not with more immediate relief almost within our grasp.

Fort Laramie had become a magic phrase to us, almost an incantation—like that of the Sioux medicine man Arrow Shield. It played over and over in our minds. Fort Laramie would have gunpowder. Fort Laramie would have food. Fort Laramie would have a smithy. Fort Laramie would have *civilization*. Fort Laramie was going to be our salvation. After Fort Laramie, nothing again would be as difficult as what had come before.

Strange how the miles seemed to be moving slower, the oxen more like snails than ever. It was becoming oppressive even to me that afternoon when Amelia stopped dead in her tracks.

"What is it, Amelia?"

She wiped the sweat dripping from her sunburned face with her rolled up dress sleeve. Her visage cleared of grime for a brief moment, I could see that the benefits of the Kennan twins' face cream had been short-lived. "In heaven's name, what is it?"

"Do you suppose there'll be any trees in Fort Laramie? I'm aching for the sight of a *real* tree. Green . . . sheltering . . . maple."

I considered as I urged the stilled oxen forward. Lazy critters. They knew the second we stopped, and stopped with us. "Make mine elm. They're much taller. I'd like them absolutely full of leaves, the way they get come midsummer back home."

Our words must have drifted back to Mama on the wagon seat, even over the creaking of the wheels. A sudden muffled sob came from her direction. Next came Papa's bark.

"Tarnation, Ruth. What are you fussing over now?"

"Home. The allover greenness of a New England

summer. There cannot possibly be trees in Fort Laramie."

I turned my head. Mama's arms were out-spread for Papa, even if he couldn't see them.

"This landscape, Henry. It cannot possibly harbor a decent tree. In hundreds of miles there have been only a few gray and dry cottonwoods, or that pitiful pine atop Scotts Bluff. The pine that was almost our daughter's undoing. *Pine*." Mama's voice turned scornful as her handkerchief dabbed over her eyes. "When has a pine needle held a candle to a full-bodied chestnut? When has a pine tree offered up nuts for roasting over a winter fire? When will I ever see a chestnut again?"

I returned my eyes to the trail ahead as Mama's sobs began in earnest. I'd never be able to feel the same scorn she did for that scraggly, ancient pine that I'd hugged. But I knew what she meant about the difference between that and a *real* tree.

I swallowed a sniffle myself as universal home-sickness spread out from our wagon like wildfire. Before we'd gone another half mile, there wasn't a dry-eyed woman in the party. Always with the exception of Miss Simpson.

True to form, Miss Simpson was shortly yelling for one of the twins to come lead her oxen. She took turns that way with us younger girls whenever she needed to "reconnoiter" or otherwise poke her nose into the affairs of her party. We'd even begun to refer to it now as the "Simpson Party" in general discussions, the way we'd started out as the "Kennan Party." Time and travel had a way of changing things like that.

Now Miss Simpson was charging down the line of toiling beasts and women, trying to locate the malefactors who'd set off this entire chain reaction. It didn't take her long to close in on us.

"Phoebe Brown, you're at the bottom of this nonsense. I know it!"

"Actually, Miss Simpson—" Amelia came to my rescue. My lovely, sunburned, protective big sister, Amelia. "You may lay the blame at my feet, Miss Simpson, not my sister's. Although it does seem to me that most of Phoebe's adventures thus far have resulted more in the aid of our party than its hindrance—"

Miss Simpson pursed her lips. "Words will be your making or your destruction someday, Amelia Brown. For the moment, however, I merely require a one-word explanation of what set off this round of self-pity, with us so close to our immediate destination."

Amelia stuck to the one word requested. *"Trees."*

"Trees. Trees?" That confused even Miss Simpson. She did a fast double-step to keep up with the progress of our animals. "Trees?"

"As in maple, elm, and chestnut. Eastern trees, Miss Simpson. *Green* trees."

"Oh."

Hands clasped behind her back, Miss Simpson furrowed her brow ferociously. She'd probably never gazed upon a tree back home except as an aid to identifying its scientific name, in Latin. Now her head rose to pivot around the treeless wilderness surrounding us.

"Haven't been any for months. Can't understand why you'd all suddenly miss them now."

"Fort Laramie," Amelia continued to explain with tremendous patience. "Fort Laramie is the ultimate, final outpost of civilization. After Laramie, there'll be nothing more to hope for. Nothing until Oregon. Surely you've invested some thought in its symbolic meaning yourself?"

"I don't deal in symbolic meanings, Miss Amelia Brown. My training was a scientific one. To me, Fort Laramie is gunpowder. Gunpowder is food—the means of a final, total reliance upon ourselves as a competent female society. Gunpowder in our hands at last will free us from the secret hope prowling my party that men—any men—will miraculously come to our aid and assistance."

"Surely such hopes aren't being seriously harbored, Miss Simpson—"

"Never mistake me for a fool. I know what I know. It's gunpowder that will set us free, Amelia Brown. Not men, and not sniveling over *trees*!"

Having stated her credo, Miss Simpson stomped back to her own team of oxen.

Yet it *was* a man of sorts who came to the aid of our still-demoralized camp that evening as we settled once more by the Platte. It was my turn to cook, and I stood by the pot, which was simmering with nothing but water, as I considered my options.

"How'd you like some lovely buffalo jerky soup, Amelia?"

"Be still, my heart."

"I thought that might be your reaction." Distastefully, I picked up a strip of the dry, stringy meat and tossed it into the water. Then another. I was going for a third when Timothy O'Malley ran up to me and tugged at my skirt.

"What is it, Timothy?"

"Visitor, Phoebe. For you. Down by the river."

"A visitor?" What kind of a visitor? Wasn't any

such *thing* as a visitor out here in the middle of nowhere. "Why doesn't the visitor come up here?"

Timothy shook his head.

"All right, then. Show me."

I trotted after the boy down to the river. Sure enough, there were visitors. Several of them. I lit up like the sun and ran for my little brother.

"Yellow Feather! You remembered me! How are you? What are you doing here?"

Of course, he couldn't really answer any of my questions, but he didn't seem to mind my hug. I finally let go of him to look up into his father's face.

"Black Tail of Hawk." I raised my right hand, showing him how nicely my blood sister wound had been healing.

"Swift Fish. We bring you present. Yellow Feather helped to hunt. His first hunt." His stern face was filled with pride as he motioned to a pack pony browsing by the river's edge. The animal was weighed down by the body of an enormous elk.

"Here. See, Swift Fish. Feel." Black Tail of Hawk took my hand to run it over the short hairs of the elk. There were several gashes in its side— one very deep, one barely penetrating the skin. I touched the smaller wound. "Yellow Feather's arrow?" I inquired.

Black Tail of Hawk thrust his shoulders back. "Yellow Feather!"

I turned to the boy, bursting with pride myself. "Good job, little brother. You will be a great hunter like your father!" I waited for that to be translated, and was rewarded with a beatific smile.

Black Tail of Hawk cleared his throat. "Yellow Feather wishes his first kill should be for Swift Fish. In his dreams his first sister has told him this."

His first sister! She had heard me atop Scotts Bluff! I kneeled down before the boy. Obviously I couldn't hug him again, not after learning he'd attained this first step to manhood. Instead, I took his right palm and rubbed it over my own. "Swift Fish thanks Yellow Feather. Swift Fish thanks Yellow Feather's first sister. I will save the hide and remember you always. Both of you."

I had to lead the laden pony into camp myself, but there was plenty of help unloading it—suddenly smiling, cheerful help. Before I returned the animal, I gave a great shout for any who hadn't caught on.

"Supper! Come and get it! But if you mangle that hide I'll have all your heads. It's mine!"

Full as I was after that feast, I managed to waddle past the exuberant campfires. I needed some advice before turning in for the night. As anticipated, Zachary Judd and Miss Prendergast were sitting sociably in Mr. Judd's wagon. It's even possible they might have been holding hands, for Miss Prendergast's shot behind her back rather quickly. Regardless, the blacksmith's face split in a grin when he spotted my head poking through the canvas opening.

"Best steak I ever et, Phoebe girl. My thanks to you."

"Wasn't me at all, but Yellow Feather and his father who were responsible. It sure is nice having a few friends out here in the wilderness. Which reminds me of my errand, Miss Prendergast. . . ."

I took a deep breath before voicing my latest request, and crossed one set of fingers, just for good measure. She'd had answers before. "I've got one prime elkskin that needs fixing. To make it soft and supple, the way the Indians do it. I was wondering if you brought along anything in your pile of books that could give me a hand?"

"Tanning. I believe that's what the process is called, Phoebe. And I seem to remember at least a few references to it in some of my journals. Why don't I hunt for the information in the morning's light?"

I badly needed that intelligence right then and

there. I was fairly anxious about that particular skin, fearing it might stiffen on me and be useless if it wasn't attended to within *minutes*. I stared back at the two of them sitting so peacefully together. I tried mightily not to jiggle with impatience. It seemed that all grown-ups—not just men—had their own timetables for things. Mr. Judd verified this truth for me.

"In the morning, girl. I won't have Alice straining her eyes in the dark."

"Yes, sir. No, sir. Thank you."

I caught Miss Prendergast when it was barely dawn. A full nine hours my elkskin had had already to turn useless on me. That was enough. If Miss Prendergast groaned at the sight of me, she didn't let on. I waited impatiently while she splashed water on her face. I helped her find her spectacles, then helped her find the proper books.

By breakfast I'd perused the available information, making out a list of materials in my head. There'd have to be a frame for the stretching, and string for the lacing. Later on there'd be call for a scraping tool. Beyond that, I'd have to find some elk brains. The directions were pretty strong about that. Brain tanning was the proper Sioux way to fix a skin. You rubbed the brains into the cleaned hide, and it softened it. According to one report from Miss Prendergast's books, the Indians claimed each animal had just enough brains in its head to tan itself nicely. The Great Spirit had ordered the world thusly.

Right off I knew it had been a mistake tossing out those elk bones beyond the camp circle the night before. Even though the brains weren't needed in the first stage of the tanning process, without them in hand I couldn't be certain that the whole skin wouldn't end up ruined. I dashed from the circle into the prairie, hunting for my elk's head. Margaret caught me at it coming back from her morning visit to a private patch of tallish grass.

"What ails you, Phoebe?"

"I can't find my head, Margaret!"

"Mercy! It's too much sun you've been getting, refusing to wear bonnets like the rest of us. It's sitting right atop your neck!"

I felt for my head, even though I knew the gesture was ridiculous. "Not *my* head, Margaret. My elk's!"

"And what would you be wanting with the poor beast's carcass?"

"Its brains! I need its brains!"

"You must, for you've certainly lost yours!

Couldn't you have held on just a wee bit longer for Laramie?"

"Margaret—" But she was already trotting back to the wagons, probably to announce that I'd mislaid my senses completely. I was about to give up the search as a lost cause, when I spotted something poking up beyond a patch of yucca. Sure enough, there was my elk skull grinning at me. Picked clean.

"Tarnation! No wonder the wolves sounded so happy last night!"

"Phoebe." Amelia was pulling at my arm. "Phoebe. Do come and have your breakfast. I won't even tell Mama you've been out here talking to yourself."

I kicked at the poor defenseless skull. "I'm not talking to myself. I was just upset over missing out on brains."

Amelia shook her head sadly. "There's still a little time before we leave, Phoebe. Perhaps you should skip breakfast and lie down. I'll ask Mrs. Hawkins to come have a look at you—"

"Enough, Amelia." I shook her arm from mine and stalked back to camp, mumbling. No one understood how important it was for me to be a proper blood sister to Yellow Feather. To be a worthy successor to his first sister. No one understood the meaning of a correctly tanned elkskin.

Through the entire morning's trek I walked sullenly, convinced my elkskin was ruined forever. I didn't even notice the strange looks I was receiving from my sister. I could hardly not notice it, however, when first Margaret, then Lizzie, and finally the Kennan twins left their oxen one by one to stroll casually past Amelia and me. It was Sarah Kennan's glances—both furtive and superior—that finally struck home.

"What are you staring at, Sarah?"

"Me? Why, la-di-da, Phoebe. I was merely taking a little constitutional."

"In the wrong direction? Back east? Surely you get enough exercise with your team."

"If I wish to walk in the wrong direction, I'm sure that's my business, Phoebe Brown."

"You're right there. The same way what I'm thinking is *my* business."

Sarah pivoted and flounced forward to her own wagon.

Amelia eyed me again. "That was somewhat discourteous, Phoebe, considering Sarah was only concerned about your well-being. Surely you've enough brains left unaddled to understand that—"

I bit back the retort I was about to lash at Amelia. She'd given me my solution, after all. "That's it! Enough brains!"

Concern spread over Amelia's face. "Phoebe, I can walk the animals by myself if you wish to rest on the wagon seat until Fort Laramie. We're really getting quite close—"

"No. No!" I skipped a few steps forward. "The books didn't say the brains had to be *elk*. They could be deer, or buffalo . . . by the time I get to that stage, we'll surely have gunpowder, surely find other game."

"What *are* you going on about, Phoebe?"

I didn't answer. My honor as a blood sister to the Sioux would remain intact. Yellow Feather and his first sister's present would be properly preserved.

Freshly buoyed and more enthusiastic than ever, I pursued my tanning project at the nooning. Another important item needed was a proper cleaning tool. As Mr. Judd was a blacksmith, I squatted inside his wagon explaining my predicament as I held a mirror before his face while he enjoyed a late shave.

"Well, Phoebe"—he scraped beneath his chin—"from what you're telling me, it seems you need a good strong handle, and a good strong blade."

I adjusted the mirror an inch. "Yes, sir, seems that way to me, too. But where do I get them?"

"Never saw such an impatient child. Takes longer than that for me to think." He scraped some more while I tried for patience.

"Seems to me—"

"Yes, Mr. Judd?"

"Seems to me I brought the blade from my old straight razor along, just in case."

"Really?"

"It also seems to me your description mentioned something about elk horn handles. You still have those antlers about?"

"Yes, sir. I kept them for souvenirs last night. Didn't have the sense to hang on to the entire head, though."

"Fetch them—"

I'd already started easing out of the wagon, the forgotten mirror still in my hand.

"—after the shaving is finished, Phoebe."

I inched back. "Yes, sir."

"Maybe I can put the two together while rolling in this wagon all day. It'd be nice having something to do with my hands."

"Thank you, Mr. Judd!"

I was prying a few boards off the side of the wagon that evening when Papa caught on.

"Is that you, Phoebe?"

I poked one eye through the newly revealed space and caught Papa's peering down at me. "Yes, sir."

"What in tarnation are you doing?"

"Giving you a little more air, Papa. Seems to me it's been getting stuffy in there recently."

I'd hunted high and low, but there just wasn't anything like lumber to be had elsewhere. And I needed my frame. Since the other necessaries seemed within hand, it struck me as time to get down to business. Step number one. Stretch the elkskin. Four little boards off the sides of the wagon couldn't do that much harm. It would be ages till we had another big river crossing to worry about. And I could always nail them back up when I was finished.

"That's thoughtful of you, daughter, but I'm not convinced air on my toes will prove that useful. Why don't you open up a piece of canvas instead?"

"Dust, Papa. Too much dust at that level. Let's just give this a try for a few days."

"I fail to see how there could be more dust several feet farther up—"

"Trust me, Papa." I pried off the fourth and final board and made my escape.

I hardly noticed those last miles to Laramie. Or the last evening before reaching our destination. All the other girls were spending every spare moment patching their most presentable frocks and gussying up their bonnets while they chattered about their hopes for the fort. As these hopes mainly involved available young men, I paid little attention. The other voices wafting around the campfires as I worked on my skin were a little harder to ignore. It was amazing how far the train's desires had gone beyond the basic need for gunpowder and flour.

Mrs. Hawkins was hoping for more than a working blacksmith. Theodore had exhausted her medical skills and now it was a doctor she was after. She was convinced there'd be one who could give an opinion on her husband's head malady. Mrs. Davis and Mrs. Russell and the younger widows scribbled fiercely over tear-dappled letters they intended to have sent back home. The possibility of spreading the facts of their bereavement to kith and kin apparently gave them great solace. Miss Prendergast made long lists of questions to ask concerning flora she'd been observing. Mrs. O'Malley had got it into her head—despite all signs to the contrary—that Mr. O'Malley was on the verge of expiring. She was praying loudly for a priest at Laramie to give her husband something she called Extreme Unction, while Gerald O'Malley was bellowing from his wagon that Last Rites were the *last* thing he needed. The youngest O'Malleys also had no doubts about their needs. Peppermint sticks would bring them eternal happiness. And Mama still wanted to see a leafy green tree, although she was willing to settle for a garden overflowing with ripe red tomatoes and crisp green peppers— preferably set within the environs of a polished, well-laid-out New England village.

As for me, I let all those wishes blow clear over my head. All my spare time was spent lacing that elkskin to its frame. The girls were long past the point of debating whether I'd gone mad or not. Now they *knew* I'd lost my senses. Let them have their little entertainment. I struggled on, poking holes around the edge of the elkskin with Mama's biggest needle. Hannah was the only one with a pertinent comment.

"In the brief time we were with the Pawnee, Phoebe—"

I didn't even bother to raise my head, just adjusted the needle in my mouth so I could speak.

"Yes?"

"During my sister's and my own brief visit, I did notice some of the women working on skins."

"And?"

"I hate to say it, but your skin doesn't look anything like theirs, Phoebe."

"Maybe they were farther along."

"Maybe." Hannah wandered away, unconvinced.

I finally got the thing strung up during the next nooning. I sank back on my haunches to admire my efforts. No doubt about it, the hide was stretched good and taut, like a Sioux drum. Yellow Feather's present was ready for its next stage. I picked up Mr. Judd's elk-handle scraper and set to. It had a nice heft, and I began to get the hang of the task just as we had to pack up and leave once more. I didn't get to work on my skin at all that night, though.

Instead, we arrived at the fort.

TWELVE

*P*hoebe, look!"

Just after the nooning on that momentous day—*Laramie Day*—Amelia nudged me out of my walking revery. I'd been trying to figure out how long it would take to actually finish the skin. And what I could do with it afterward. It would make a nice wall hanging in Oregon, or a rug. Then again, a buckskin dress like Yellow Feather's mama had worn would be impressive. Although one skin might not be quite enough for that. Particularly as mine appeared to have shrunk somewhat in the early stages of the curing process.

"Phoebe!"

"What is it, Amelia?" I finally focused on her pointing finger. "Oh. Those shacks over there. They're in Miss Prendergast's guidebook. Fort Bernard . . . set up by some mountain men trying to compete with Laramie. Fairly rough, though. Two walls aren't even finished yet."

Come to think of it, an Indian dress made more sense. I lapsed back into my private world for a few more miles, wondering if and when we got the gunpowder at Laramie I'd be able to bag another elk.

"Phoebe, look!"

"What is it *now*, Amelia?"

This time it was a vast Indian camp, just beginning about a half mile in front of us. From the signs of tipis poking through the clear air it looked to go on a fair ways.

"That must be the rendezvous Yellow Feather and his people were heading for. It does seem as if every clan they're related to is waiting for them."

That woke me up for a while. I tried to see if I could pick out Black Tail of Hawk's tipi somewhere, but there really were too many tipis, and all of them too far off. I returned to designing that elkskin dress in my mind. How would Yellow Feather's first sister have decorated hers? There'd be fringes, for sure, and some of those fancy trade beads we'd brought along—

"For heaven's sake, Phoebe!"

"Now what, Amelia?"

"Over there! You can see Laramie!"

"That's nice."

Amelia precipitously left her post next to the oxen and disappeared. I thought nothing of it till she returned with a surprise—half a skin of water that she carefully upended over my head. That woke me up.

"Amelia," I spluttered. "Amelia, what has gotten into you?"

"*Me?* What has gotten into *you*, Phoebe? You've practically faded from the living since you took on that silly elkskin."

"It is *not* silly! It's special! It was a gift from—" From whom, really? Yellow Feather, among the living, or his first sister, among the spirits? I shook my head. I wasn't atop the heights of Scotts Bluff anymore. I was down here on the prairie, alive. I shook some more and began to laugh. Yellow Feather's first sister would want nothing more than for me to be *alive*. "You could have a point, Amelia. Did you say that was Fort Laramie? That sort of dried mud thing up ahead?"

"Anything else it might be, Phoebe?"

"Nope. We've passed all the other landmarks. We've used up all the miles, six hundred and fifty of them." I let out a whoop.

"It's *Laramie*, Amelia!"

We met for a hug and did a little jig right there. You'd think that might have spooked the oxen, but it didn't. For a wonder it didn't even make them stop and stare. They were too set at this late time of the day in getting to the river water they smelled up ahead.

It was dark by the time Miss Simpson led us directly up to the front gates of the fort. A sentry leaned over the palisades.

"Fort's closed till morning. And you can't camp by the front gates like that. You'll have to make for that free grass half a mile to the south. The Sioux took up all the other good spots." He squinted through the dark, then reached for a lantern to hold over the edge of the parapet. "Say, ain't you—" The sentry turned around and roared.

"Harley! Michaels! Lookit this! It's that female train them Injuns was goin' on about. It's the *Petticoat Party!*"

Miss Simpson tried raising her voice to contradict that appellation, but it was too late. A band of riffraff had clambered up to the palisades to see for themselves. By the light of their lamps their scruffiness was apparent, and took on new dimensions. Long beards and wild hair were outlined in the night. Timothy O'Malley began to screech in fright.

"That's enough!" Miss Simpson bellowed. "Turn your wagons for the campsite, women!"

By morning's light Fort Laramie held a certain appeal. It sat upon a modest bluff over the Laramie River. Sun gleamed on its white adobe walls. Those walls must have been fifteen feet tall. It wasn't all that tall, of course, but the wooden palisade and the blockhouse over the main gate added height to effect. After all, we'd seen nothing this high since long before Independence. Nothing man-made.

Down below the bluff, edging the river and off for a mile or more to the east were the Indian camps. Tens of thousands of Indians it seemed, more than even Hannah and Sarah could wish for.

Amelia caught me staring and dragged me back for breakfast. It was the last of Yellow Feather's elk, but we didn't linger over that, either. There was too much to be done this day. Stock had to be taken to the fort for shoeing. Some of the wagons needed new wheel rims and axle repairs. Supplies had to be replenished.

Most of all, we were itching to see other civilized human beings. Not that I'd classify the few sorry specimens we'd spied last night in that category.

The *Petticoat Party*. That did rankle some.

"For goodness sake, finish your meal so we may go to the fort, Phoebe."

"Yes, Mama." I ate the last bite. "Did you find the coins in the cherry dresser, Mama?"

"I did." She carefully doled out a few to me. "Amelia and I will see to the shoeing, Phoebe. You're to be in charge of provisions. Do be cautious."

"Yes, Mama."

"Don't let them hornswoggle you, Phoebe!"

I poked my face into the gap between boards in the wagon's side. "I won't, Papa. Sorry you can't come, Papa."

Papa growled.

I walked through the main gate by the blockhouse expecting something. Something special to repay us for the pain and the distance. Something to make up for that trench of bodies we'd left over four hundred miles back. Not Mama's New England village. No. It ought to be something considerably more impressive. It ought to be like the hold of a castle, at the least, with maybe one of those Gothic cathedrals thrown in, stained-glass windows sparkling in the sun.

What met my scrutiny instead was a great, dusty, open space filled with milling livestock. Surrounding this courtyard were the walls of the fort itself. Built into those walls were long rows of dirty hovels. And the occupants weren't dressed in velvet and ermine, either. I'd seen cleaner Indians. Much cleaner.

Taking in the broader view that way, I tripped right over the outstretched legs of a long-bearded wilderness man lodged up against the nearest wall, liquor jug in hand.

"Watch where you're goin', yer Ladyship!"

"Pardon me, I'm sure!"

Behind me, Mama and Amelia were leading Buck and Bright. I watched them take in the same sights I had; watched their faces fall. Buck stumbled over the same whiskey-sodden man that I had. Curses—more impressive than any Papa had ever conceived—filled the air. Mama turned white and apologized profusely, while Amelia prodded our beasts toward the smoking fires of the smithy.

I sighed and squared my shoulders. Maybe I'd been guilty of harboring some of those unmentionable secret thoughts Miss Simpson had brought up. About *men*—knights in shining armor—coming to our party's rescue. Men chivalrous enough to volunteer to lead our train over the rest of the desert and mountains beyond Laramie. Men to take over the strain of work and worry gallantly, but not cavalierly. I shook my head clear of that fantasy.

On a much more practical level I *knew* I'd been

guilty of attaching civilized hopes to this obviously uncivilized place. Listening to the yearnings of our women for days could do that to a person.

A wad of well-used chewing tobacco flew past me, just catching the tip of my right boot. I kicked it away distastefully and examined the hovels. One had a hand-lettered sign in front. SUPLIES, it read.

That missing *p* was the last straw. I knew then and there our Petticoat Party was going to have to finish up those last fourteen hundred miles on our own steam, because no bunch of drunken, unwashed, illiterate males was going to give us aid and succor. I'd learned to do plenty of other things on this journey. I'd even made it to the top of Scotts Bluff. I'd teach myself to shoot and hunt, too, by heaven. So would the rest of our women. We'd survived as far as Laramie, hadn't we? All we needed were the necessaries.

I marched into the dark "suplies" building. A scrawny individual glanced up from an account book on the counter. He gave me a sort of three-toothed smile as he patted down the greasy strings of his shoulder-length hair.

"As I live and breathe. One of them Petticoat Party females. Eat up all your men for breakfast, did you?"

I glowered.

He hardly noticed, he was that pleased with his humor. "What'll you have, Missy?"

"Gunpowder. *Dry* gunpowder, please. And lots of it!"